Lock Down Publications and Ca$h
Presents

THE
Dirty Side Of
MONEY

Scheming, Scamming,
& Grinding

Written By
PRINCE
Gritty and Raw Urban/Street Crime Author

First Edition 2025

Printed in the United States of America

This is a work of fiction. Names, characters, places, and incidents either
are products of the author's imagination or are used fictitiously. Any
similarity to actual events or locales or persons, living or dead, is
entirely coincidental.

Lock Down Publications
P.O. Box 944
Stockbridge, GA 30281
www.lockdownpublications.com

Like our page on Facebook: Lock Down Publications
www.facebook.com/lockdownpublications.ldp

Stay Connected with Us!

Text **LOCKDOWN** to 22828 to stay up-to-date with new releases, sneak peaks, contests and more…

Like our page on Facebook:
Lock Down Publications

Join Lock Down Publications/The New Era Reading Group

Visit our website:
www.lockdownpublications.com

Follow us on Instagram:
Lock Down Publications

Email Us: We want to hear from you!

Prologue

Montell stroked hard and pounded deep in the pussy in missionary. He popped his shit to Verena, too, like he was known to pop. "Ah, yeah, bitch! I told yo ass, once you finally start giving a nigga this pussy, you wasn't gonna stop! Didn't I tell you! Huh! Didn't I! Now look at you! Look at you! Got yourself all caught up in my world and don't even know how to stop loving this shit! Now do you? Take this dick! Take it! 'Cause I'mma give it to ya rough every time from here on!" he said to her, working like a madman, digging in and stroking properly between the legs of his freak fanatic.

Montell wasn't quite ready to nut just yet, but Verena, she was desperate to get her first one off. She burned with fire and desire to cream all over his dick.

"I'm all caught up in your world, because this the world where I wanna be," she let out between pants. "This dick feels so good to me, Montell. Keep fucking me like you doing. And make them monster faces for me you always do." Verena talked back dirty.

Montell's rhythm got even more ferocious. He had no apologies in the way he fucked her. "Yo freaked out ass! You done turnt out to be a nympho, I see! But I'mma be honest with you. I probably wanted this pussy more than you wanted this dick I'm giving you. Am I lying? Huh!" He spoke more dirty antics to her in between his strokes and pants now. They had gotten accustomed to be chatty a bit while fucking. Dude was putting in work.

"Yes daddy! That's a lie. And guess what? You told it. Because I wanted the dick more today than *ever* before. I had to have it!" Verena declared. She began to grunt and moan in a way like she was speaking in a *"Holy tongue."* The challenging bantering continued as they fucked on.

"No, hell! I think it's me who wanted it more. I'm the lucky nigga today."

He humped harder and faster at this point. It was like he was a sex deprived Pitbull on a hot piece of ass. His hardcore mode had set in. This nigga was on one.

"Ooh, Maurice!" Verena screamed his name ecstatically. Thankfully, no one else was around. Their little secret fuck session could've been exposed behind her outburst. "Give it to me, boy! Keep hitting it just like this." She egged him on as if he was a gladiator in battle, going in hard for the throne. Victory was his to be claimed. This nigga felt destined to be the *"Crown Prince"* and *"King of the Hill,"* the best to have ever done it at the prison on such a level. Maybe the first and only.

"Come on. Let's switch it up for a little while. I wanna hit this pussy from the back. I wanna see you cream all over my dick as I slide in and outta you," Montell said confidently. He was a heavyweight in the manhood department, and fucking doggy-style, was his favorite position. Dude was eager to pull out slowly, and then, slam back into her pussy ferociously, to work a slow exit and fast entry mode of strokes. "Shit! Talking about you being a nympho... the muthafuckin' freak done came outta my ass! This nigga right here!" His build up was unbelievable.

Montell took his right thumb and popped it into her booty hole to increase her level of stimulation. This trick worked instantly.

"Ooh Maurice! Damn this feels good, too! Where you learn this at, boo! It's like something was added to go along with the dick. It feels so good to me, baby! Please... please I said... fuck me in my ass now, will you? Fuck me in my ass like you fucking me in this pussy, baby! I want it, and I want it now!" She begged.

***

Eventually, Montell slowly withdrew the dick from the juice-box, taking notice of how heavily coated it was with the cream of Verena's orgasm. He got what he was looking for. It was a small victory added to all his other accomplishments. They had an intimate banter again there between repositioning. "Now this what the fuck I'm talkin' 'bout! Look at how I make you nut when we fuck! In the beginning, you didn't even wanna give a nigga the pussy. What kinda shit was that!"

"The kinda shit that's called... making yo ass work for it, nucca."

"And worked for it. I did, didn't I," he came back with, adding a wide smile.

"Indeed. But my question to you is... was it worth it?"

"Hell, fuck yeah, it was! I couldn't have asked for a better opportunity," he said.

He then palmed both her ass-cheeks, parted them wide to make easy access into her tightest delicate love hole, and situated his dick's head at the entry of her sensitive love spot. There was a trio to choose from: *pussy, mouth and ass!* Montell wanted to explore them all.

Not that he needed extra lubrication, but he was always in the habit of spitting on his dick in these type moments, to make entry easier into either a pussy or a female's asshole. This was what he did, gliding smoothly into Verena's back door, penetrating fully.

This bitch clean as ever, he thought. *Something like them "stool-less virgin females" that the Holy Qur'an and other Islamic material for Muslim males mention will be rewarded to men who are doers of good and granted "Paradise." I done read and studied this in my days. Or, maybe, this was* the "spiritual lyrics of the Holy Qur'an" quote that that nigga 2Pac spoke on in his song, Bomb First? It's all too similar, he thought.

Montell learned of this through his reading of Muslim books. He felt like his access had already been approved. This motherfucker really enjoyed fucking Verena how he saw fit.

The boogeyman bad boy Montell banged this half sophisticated yet wannabe ghetto fabulous bitch in the ass a few good minutes before getting back to the basics with stroking seriously in the pussy. They didn't have long. This was because they were on the clock. And her special request to be fucked in the ass, was for extra credit. Something she'd been almost dying to experience. If not but once. She finally got it.

Verena said to Montell, "All those damn porn videos I done watched over the years had me eager to have my backside blown out in this way."

"Say whaaaat! No-they-didn't!" He smiled and laughed at her simultaneously.

"Oh yes-they-did, too!" She responded, now smiling widely herself.

With one last re-positioning to missionary again, Montell got rough with her like she wanted and put Verena in the "Buck."

"Well go ahead then, Montell! With your bad self, boy. Do your thing, sweetheart! Beat down deep in this pussy and get aggressive like you know how to. I won't tell if you won't," she playfully let out and grin mischievously.

There was something unforgettable about the moment. For them both. It was like he was the heavyweight champ, and no doub, he'd worked his way through the ranks to become this. Montell was Dat Nigga indeed. If only for those few minutes he had when he fucked Verena. It was all worth it.

**

The life of an inmate was amazing for the time being. Montell was getting money, and this nigga was fucking good too. Their experience with anal sex was appreciated. It was his third time and only her first. Might it also be said that of this particular taboo, he found a conquering surge of energy with it. One he hadn't felt in quite a long time.

Dude was the motherfucking man! And, a man on top of his game. And although a convict, Montell had boss-like status and clout. He maintained his shit airtight. The way he was supposed to.

PART ONE

Chapter 1

Two Months Later...

Montell toyed around with a gift he was given—fondling the buttons and tapping the screen of the extraordinary gadget he held. He had become more than fascinated at how magnificent and mesmerizing the latest model *Apple iPhone* truly was. With the newest technology it held, he was sure to be pleased.

Damn! These muthafuckas' get better and better each year, don't they, he thought. The phone was a present. Something to remember the times with. It came from his highly infatuated and dick craving chick he once worked for at the prison, before she resigned. He was an orderly for her—Verena—inside the facility. They both were excited about each other and had gotten deeply involved. At least in the beginning, from a feelings and emotional standpoint.

This grew to something stronger, along with all else included when a male and female make a passionate love connection. A connection that they had carried on for the better part of a year and a half off and on. Good for the most part, as the two envisioned a prosperous future ahead of them. One they'd striven for and wanted to live out to the best of their abilities. At least this was how Montell felt. And, he did everything possible to see to it that this was to become a reality. He was eager to balance out the thug in him with the gentleman he wanted to become. In totality. A polished individual.

*"Look, Verena, ever since the day I convinced you that I
was the type of nigga who could keep my muthafuckin' mouth
closed and my business to myself, you gave in to me more
and more with every conversation, right?"*

"Right."

*"And our bond was made solid over time with me backing
up my words, right?"*

"You right with that, too."

*"And not only that, you think highly of me. Am I right
about this, too?"*

"You are."

*"But to be honest, this shit became apparent, that my style
and swag, fit whatever standards and other shit you was
looking for in a nigga,"* he said to her in one of the
conversations before they weren't able to have a
conversation anymore.

The bitch in Verena was a side to her that Montell never
thought or knew existed. Hell, they all have it in them.
Women that is. Verena just hid hers better than those he'd
known.

*"You appealed to me differently, Montell. This was one of
the reasons I made a choice to deal with you. I missed the
street shit I was enthralled with from my ex in high school. A
thug like him and now you was what I always wanted again.
It was a long time coming."* She replied to his words.

It was through practice and his careful attention to detail
of what she said and how she said it that played the key role
in helping Montell catch her. He eventually was able to
persuade her to get down with the program he had long been
on. She was money hungry anyhow. And Montell, was a
scamming nigga on the move mentally, trying to find a way
to scam more. He was always looking to get over on the
government.

Although book smart and penny-wise, nonetheless, this
nigga was from the streets and knew how the game goes. He
just acted and talked different than the normal street dudes

did. But once he caught Verena and had her for sure, he was able to make her join him with what he really had in mind. He wanted to scheme hard this time and get some more money. This was how it all came to be.

***

From The Beginning...

Montell finished a Federal bid for income tax fraud, money laundering, and tax evasion, amongst other things. He was released to the custody of the Georgia Department of Corrections, the penal system of his home state. There was state-related convictions as well. But, It was to be no supervision once free. Montell would completely be discharged if he'd understood his sentence correctly.

His start in the peach state was at Phillips State Prison in Buford, Georgia, where he qualified as a law clerk.

"Look, if possible, could y'all give me a job in the law library, please? If that's not asking too much. I got a degree to litigate. And, when I was in the feds, this was the work I did. My profile shows it," he said to the board members who classified him. His credentials checked out. He was granted his first detail in state lock-up.

Montell eventually worked his way up the trustee ladder. He became the *Chief Administrative Aide* for the superintendent there, an African American warden, a female that had a nice ass and other physical qualities. Mostly from her days of youth.

This bitch got it going on, he thought at first glance, laying eyes on her instantaneously. Verena Evette Gordon was the lady of the hour.

Verena, stood at five foot six and weighed maybe a hundred fifty-five pounds. There were no signs of fast aging. Verena had energy, flare, and a unique appearance. She could've gone for twenty-two, although she was thirty-eight years of age. Her sex appeal and *femme fatale* attraction went hand-in-hand with the attitude she had. It took a lot for a female to be in control over hundreds of males. But she managed well. Then along came a spider, a nigga named Montell, talking that talk and walking that walk. He was a special kind of thug though. Exclusive even. Corporate, so to speak. And passionate as ever.

Verena's fabulous set of 36 double D's and plump ass enticed him. If he had to say so himself, this particular *Verena,* made his dick get hard just like the middle-aged Serena Williams did, the pro tennis phenom in her prime, in her cat suit.

Verena Gordon was raised well but yearned for excitement in a man and with a man. Opposite her athletic skills, she was a straight-A student coming of age. Verena was awarded a scholarship. One she gladly accepted upon graduating high school. *Spelman* took her in. This was a plus. She didn't want to be distant from her mother, who was an elderly lady, and needed her daughter around.

Verena let Montell know one day, "I earned degrees in Criminal Justice and Social-Science," she boasted. Adding, "And the closest to a sibling I ever had was my best friend, Tiffany. This the only one person I've always shared *everything* with. Clothes, food, deeds, you name it. And *everything,* means *everything.* "

Tiffany D. Long worked for Verena at the prison. She was her personal secretary.

Chapter 2

Montell had a conversation with a homie of his one night. A dude named Eric Mickens. This was not long after getting to the prison. Eric himself hadn't long gotten out of the feds. He and Montell and three others were on the same indictment.

"Yo Eric, check this, my nigga. How 'bout, we got this fine ass bitch for a warden over the prison I'm at now," he said, making his friend aware of the attractive lady he saw almost on a daily.

"Word! Hell, for *you* to say it, and to put it the way you did, she has to be a baddie! What she look like, though?"

"Shid, nigga, the better question should be, what do I plan to do to get her to pay me some attention?" Montell responded. "That's what you *should've* asked."

"I know that's right, nigga. Because we the type of niggaz, who feel like we can have any bitch in the world we want. *Any* bitch, you know!" the friend proclaimed.

"Bro, *I'm* the type of nigga who *can* have any bitch I want," Montell said, always putting himself first. "And, she's one of them types I could fuck with. But, to answer your question... shorty is a tight piece of work. She's fit. Flat stomach, firm thighs, and got a apple bottom round ass. A bit *bougie but* still can get it."

"If that's the case then, nigga... how many times you done locked her in your imagination and jacked ya dick thinking about her?" he worded with a solid laugh.

"Oh! That! I done knocked the bitch off like three times already since I been here! That pussy know it's good too, nigga! And I think she's pregnant by me now!" Montell let out. His imagination was something serious, as is *ALL* inmates' imagination when it concerned a sexy female.

"Ha-ha!" Eric laughed like crazy at his words.

The two continued to laugh wildly, knowing exactly how hard dick convicts think. The imagination and ways of thinking of an inmate, is something else altogether. Over everything, survival and getting a piece of pussy, is all that niggaz on lock think about every day. Nothing else really mattered above a female and survival.

Montell continued, "But truth be, bro, this warden bitch, Verena Gordon, is the total package of a chick. She got style, grace, and a lot of ambition to match her personality. From how she presents herself, she'll make many women feel bad about themselves in any situation. I'm talkin' 'bout the ones who only dream in envy of having what Verena has."

"And what's that?"

"Shit! I'm more than sure, by her working for the state, she gotta be financially straight. The bitch looks like she's got money from somewhere. Her daddy maybe. A deceased husband's pension money. A lawsuit settlement. Something! Not to mention the benefits she has at her behest by being an official of the State. She's articulate and got authoritative rule. And let's not forget the respect she's earned. I just got a job with her, and don't really know too much just yet. I will soon enough though."

"Montell. That's a mouth full there, my nigga. And how you know all this?"

"It's because, nigga... like I just said, I got a job working for the bitch, bro. I wrote her a letter about a detail in her area. She approved. And, once I found out what her whole name was, I started snooping around on her social media pages. That's how."

"Oh! That's how? So, you did your homework, I see."

"Fuck yeah, I did, nigga! You know me, I'll be a muthafuckin' fool to let a opportunity like this pass me by, to not try and find a way to finesse a bitch to fuck with me. That's just my nature. And as a man, I gotta at least attempt something. That'll make me a pussy if I didn't. On God, it would," he stated.

"Word, bro. I'm feeling you on that. But do she got any kids? A stable man in her life? Any of that shit?"

"Hell, I don't know. I gotta check into all that to see. But it really don't matter if she do. And if anybody, I'mma keep *you* informed on everything. Besides, I got a way to get all the information we could use on these other niggaz who locked up here with me. We can probably cash in on the income tax hustle again, or from some other hustle we could capitalize on with the personal information of these suckas."

"Now that part was what I next had in mind to talk about," responded Eric.

He'd gotten an urgent text message from his twin sister, Nasha. Something chaotic was happening with her and she needed his assistance. Immediately!

Nasha: *Eric! It's an emergency, bruh! Get here to my house ASAP! It's serious! I can't say over the phone!*

Eric: *Nasha, WTF! I'm on the way now!*

"Yo Mo, I gotta bounce, my nigga! My sister just hit me up talking 'bout I need to get to her crib ASAP! I'll hit you back some other time, homie. Or you hit me back one," dude stated to the incarcerated friend.

"That's what's up, my nigga. Handle ya business, bro. And tell Nasha I said what up too. But check that. We can get up another time."

"Word!"

The call came to an abrupt end. The two were in the process of talking up ways of coming upon different money-making schemes they could utilize to scam again. But this time, to get some serious bread. Not piece meal takings throughout the year, but large jobs to get lump sums at one time. Because not a day goes by that scammers aren't busy churning up scams. The text message from Eric's sister brought this to a close. At least for now.

***

Meanwhile...

Eric raced out the front door of his place en route across town to the SWATS, also known as Southwest Atlanta Suburbs where his sister and her fourteen-year-old daughter Zakeya, and the high-level drug dealing boyfriend of hers named Keno all lived. While driving, he called Nasha back, so to kinda gain a sense of the true nature of all that was going on in her household. What was it that needed him there ASAP! What was the shit she couldn't say over the phone? His heart pounded.

She answered, "How far away are you, bruh? Please... get here now!"

"I'm on the way now, sis! I'm almost there. What the fuck going on? I don't wanna walk blindly into something!"

"Bruh! I had to pop this nigga ass, foo!"

"Huh! Who? What nigga?"

"Keno! He did some really foul shit, my nigga! You'll see when you get here. Just hurry the fuck up, will you!"

"Just calm down for now until I get there, okay."

"I'll try. Just get here!" Nasha lastly stated then killed the call.

Eric knew then and there that the reality of the situation had to be serious. He sped up. Panic began to set in, but not in totality to where it would cause him to no longer be able to think properly.

Nearly twenty-five minutes later, he was pulling up in Nasha's driveway. Her 300 Series Mercedes Benz and Keno's 500 Series Benz were parked inside the garage. The doors to the garage were up. Nasha noticed the lights from Eric's car beam brightly through the windows of the house.

She ran to open the door to let him in. He hopped out his car and speed-walked to the front entrance.

"What the fuck, Nasha!" he exclaimed.

Tears were heavy in her eyes. She was shaking uncontrollably.

"Here, bruh! In the bedroom." She managed to let out, grabbing Eric by the arm and they hurried inside, heading straight to the master suite.

Eric put eyes on the seriously wounded boyfriend who lay on the bed. He'd been shot three times in the upper body. However, he wasn't dead just yet. Barely living. Dude was still breathing, squirming, and struggling to speak. He coughed up blood.

"Nasha! What the fuck this shit all about? You already know I ain't long got outta prison!" Eric let out loudly. "And gimme that muthafuckin' gun!" He'd just taken notice of it in her hand. She had it present all along.

Nasha complied, passing Eric the nine-millimeter Glock pistol she'd shot Keno with.

"Bruh! I found out that this bitch-ass nigga, been fucking my goddamn daughter on the low!"

"What! No! Ain't no way!"

"And how 'bout, this bastard, done fucked around and got my muthafuckin' daughter pregnant too! She ain't but fourteen, my nigga! You know this ain't right!"

Keno attempted to mumble out something to the effect of, "You gonna pay for this shit, bitch. On God, you is. As soon as my brother and 'em try to call me, and I ain't picking up. And as soon as I get right again."

"Nigga, fuck you!" she vehemently spat.

"Nasha, how you know this shit true?" asked Eric.

"Because, bro, I had my phone linked to some hidden cameras I had installed in the house, and to the TVs everywhere. One in here," she pointed to the 80-inch smart TV, "And one there," then to a spot up high in the corner of the ceiling. "I put one in Zakeya's room. Her TV was linked to my phone too. And, I had another one planted in the living room, and in the den. I saw this fuck-nigga with my own eyes, bruh, raping my goddamn daughter! What the fuck!"

Nasha was given time to do all this when Keno had not long before the day went on a re-up run over to Texas. He had a Mexican supplier.

"So why yeen say something ahead of time?"

"It's because, I wanted to wait 'til the right time to strike! And then... I got his ass! Pussy-nigga!" She vehemently spat. "And I couldn't go to the police. That would've caused them to look into other shit. Things that I'm definitely involved in."

"True." Eric uttered then turned to have a look at the wounded boyfriend victim. "But damn! What the fuck, Keno! How could you, nigga!"

"Fuck both y'all!" He spat in defiance then coughed. "I'mma have both you muthafuckas whacked!" He coughed again, more blood came up.

"Bruh! We simply can't let this pussy live to see another day. He gonna come back and get us. It ain't no way, my nigga! So, what we gonna do? We gotta do something." Nasha muttered, looking on at her twin with a serious face, nostrils flared, and blood in her eyes.

"Yeah, you right. Something gotta give. We can't let him get right and then come back to take us out the game. I done seen too many muthafuckas' who got killed in the same way, because they did something to somebody, and let 'em come back and get 'em. Or pulled a gun on a muthafucka' and didn't pop shit! So, what we gonna do about this nigga here? This is what we gonna do about him," the Twin spat.

He then slowly raised the gun, trained it at Keno's head, grimaced with an evil face, and pulled the trigger.

BANG!

Keno's head whip backwards, now flat onto the pillow, never moving again. Blood, brain splatter, and bone fragments plastered the pillow. The instant smell of death took precedent over the atmosphere of the room. It was a strong stench of urine and loose bowels. His body had released its waste.

The problems Nasha once faced with her daughter being repeatedly molested by the now murdered boyfriend, Keno, along with Keno himself becoming a problem because he'd been caught, was no more. Eric had *murked* him then and there on the spot.

A tear rolled down Eric's face. He'd killed a man. At no time in his life had he imagined he'd have to resort to doing such a thing. But he did. And he couldn't take it back. Also, at the same time, he never thought he had it in him to take it this far, to get gangsta and blast a nigga from the face of the earth. *It is what it is. It just is what it is is,* he said twice over in his own mind. *Come what may. I did what was necessary.*

Chapter 3

After seconds of silence, Eric and Nasha began contemplating on how they would get rid of the body. But before they were to reveal to one another the best way they individually saw fit, Eric needed to assure himself that their secret would be kept safe among each other. Or else, they'd both have hell to pay.

"Look, Nasha, you already know that this some serious shit here. Ain't no need for me to make you aware of the consequences we both now face, if this shit ever gets out."

"So, we ain't gonna call the police to let them know what happened?"

"Fuck no! If we do that, we may as well just gone on to fucking prison then!"

"Bruh, we can dress it up and make it seem like the nigga was beating on me and tried to kill me—"

"And then what? Your brother, who's a convicted felon who not long ago just got outta prison, a ex con came over here to your house, pulled out a gun that he not supposed to have anyway, and shot and killed dude to stop him from beating on you, the nigga's on-again off-again girlfriend! *Dafuq!* Nah, Nasha! We can't call the police. Ain't no way we can do that. We can't let this shit get out. We gotta cover it up and then live with it for the rest of our lives."

"But what we gonna do when his brother and their family start coming by here looking for him?"

"You ain't seen him. Y'all broke up again weeks ago and y'all haven't talked since."

"That sounds good. But what if they don't believe me and try to dig deeper and shit?"

"Just continue telling 'em the same story."

"Gotcha. Now how we plan to get rid of this nigga's ass?"

"We got fortune on our side. Luckily for us, we got a uncle who owns a funeral home. A funeral home that I helped pay for."

"That's right. Uncle Charles and his funeral home. But, how's he gonna make the body disappear?"

"Cremate, sis. He's gonna burn the nigga up! Then, I'll have Uncle Charles flush the ashes down the toilet then and there." He then paused.

He gave Nasha a hard look eye-to-eye and wanted to be sure that she knew that he really meant business and was for real with what he was now about to say. Dude was serious as he'd ever been.

"Nasha, look, we got secrets now. Okay."

In a somber tone, she responded, "I know. And we gotta now float together, or we drown together. That's the bottom line."

"We got secrets that bind us together." "Every relationship, every set of siblings has secrets."

"You're right about that, sis. But not like this one." He extended his right hand. "Pinky promise."

"Pinky promise, bruh. To the death of us," she came back with.

They interlocked fingers and gazed seriously at one another. Eric then pulled out his phone and made the contact to their uncle. The mortician answered and they talked.

***

Weeks Later...

Montell might've had a bit of luck on his side when it came to Verena. All he had to do was play it well and handle his business properly. With her, there were two major obstacles that stood in her path and prevented her from reaching complete feminine atonement. The type every accomplished woman strived to have.

Verena was without a man in her life. And not only this, but she also desperately wanted to have a child or two by the time her biological clock ticked out. At that point, her reproductive system would be virtually useless. She greatly feared the thought of living in *no man's land*. This became a well stated phrase the famed YouTube star Kevin Samuels coined and liked to use to describe single hopeless romantic women, black women particularly between the ages of thirty-nine and sixty.

Within one of her moments throughout the many in-depth conversations she and Montell held, Verena slipped up and revealed these fears to him.

"You got any kids?" he asked.

"No, I don't. I do wanna have a child or two though. At least at some point before I'm not able to."

"What you talkin' 'bout? Hell, I know if Janet Jackson was able to have a baby at *fifty*, then you should be able to at..." His words trail off. He was trying to get her to reveal her age without asking flat out.

"I'm forty, Montell. If you must know," she said

He looked on at her and smiled. He knew that she knew what he was up to, but she didn't mind playing tag along. A little witty banter has never hurt nobody.

Without hesitation, Montell began trying to figure out how to explore all possible angles he could to capitalize on her vulnerability and appeal to her yearnings. He wanted to gain her interest at her heart and at spirit. He figured there could be a possibility. His plan was to take his best shot at some point soon. He made progress day by day.

Chapter 4

In The Meantime . . .

Verena asked, "Montell, what you do to come to prison to begin with? That's what I'm curious to know." Of course, she was the warden, so she already knew the truth about everything. Her thing was that she wanted to see would he tell a lie about his situation or would he not? *Maybe I could fuck with him if he ain't a lier*, she thought.

He was busy cleaning up her office, one of his duties as her orderly.

"You wanna know what I got locked up for," he let out, now getting into the conversation. "Let me see, what the fuck! Ain't you the warden?" He said with a slight laugh.

"Obviously. But it's a reason why I asked *you* specifically."

"Oh, it is, you say? Okay. Cool. But, I'mma answer you. Although I'm sure you already done checked out my profile to know the reasons."

"I have. But reading it on paper ain't nothing like hearing it directly from the horse's mouth, if you know what I mean." She stated with a sly smile about her face.

"Is that right."

"Very much so. But I won't interrupt you again. Now tell me."

"No problem. I was convicted of what that fuck-ass prosecutor considered an *'elaborate money-making scheme'* put together by *'a band of hoodlums'*... niggaz was what that crack really wanted to say," Montell stated. "He said that me and my niggaz, manipulated the American financial system, and that we fucked over *Uncle Sam*, and we needed to pay. And pay we did. My charges was for federal income tax fraud, aggravated identity theft, money laundering, federal banking violations, and mortgage fraud. And my troubles with Georgia, was for identity fraud and state tax violations. But to be honest with you with how I feel about myself, I just happened to be a nigga who got a decent level of intelligence, a lot of promise, a lot of potential, and the mindset to pull off the moves that was made by me and my homies. These moves, of course, were established on the strength of us being real with one another, and to having success and money. Desperation basically." Montell expounded with a flare of confidence.

Verena sat and internalized everything graciously.

No doubt he was the type of dude who was all about TYPE, and he craved the finer things in life. There was a phrase he loved to say, *"Why should white guys have all the fun?"* Quoting the legendary Black business mogul, Reginald Lewis. Montell would remind himself of this all the time.

And also, of these words he said further to Verena. "In the words of my grandmother, *'I'm smarter than I look,'* and I'm determined to live up to those words, the ones I love to repeat to myself, and of my grandmother's words. Rather that be legally or illegally," he declared.

Chapter 5

The two—Montell and Verena—was at it again with yet another talk one day. She was curious like before, and, like always, now wanted to know how he was raised coming up, so she asked to see how truthful he'd be about this. He obliged and related his background.

"I was born to Janice Wilson and a dude named Kirk McNeal. My birthday is in early October."

"So, you're a Libra, I see."

"Oh yeah! The seventh sign in the universe and the greatest! We make the world go 'round," he let out with a chuckle.

"Um-hmm. That's debatable but tell me more about you. I wanna hear things from your mouth. You seem so passionate and determined."

"I most definitely am. But, I'm a two *hunnid* pound six-foot nigga, as you see. And I got a big dick!" He was motivated to say that part with emphasis.

Montell wanted to play the feel game with Verena. So, he only gave her the basics about himself. She was amused at his witty antics. He caused her to smile and laugh simultaneously.

He continued. "What you see is what you get. Nothing more, nothing less."

"Looks that way to me too. I can go for that," she complimented, disguising it as a remark. He caught the hint and smiled more.

"A lot of people say my appearance makes me look like I'm a Nubian dude from Sudan somewhere, or a Arab nigga. But I pride myself on being capable of attracting females of my choice, no matter their status in the world."

"So, which one are you? Either you're cocky or confident? Which one?"

"Both!" Montell came back with.

She smiled harder.

"But from me to you, I feel that if I wanted *any* woman," *including you,* he thought, "I could put in the work necessary to have them. By any means available."

"You're good. But don't flatter yourself too much with that. To some people, it may come off as arrogance," Verena cautioned.

Montell internalized her words this time and pressed on with relating himself. This wasn't the first time he'd heard that, and it may not be the last either. He felt as though Verena placed value and appreciation on cocky dudes and on confident men in this order, since it was how she said it. *But all the better, if a nigga is "cocky and confident,"* he further thought. *I'm capable of being both.*

She may have given him the prescription to the medicine required to heal her lonely heart. Montell definitely caught the hint.

As for his personal preference in appearance, Montell sometimes wore a well shaved bald head. It shined brighter than the capitol building downtown Atlanta on a sunny day. The dome of the structure is gold-plated and reflected the rays of the sun with a blinding effect. But he recently went back to growing his hair again and having waves. The bald head was for reasons of discipline. Anytime he was in a militant mindset. Not anymore.

Montell was a well-groomed man, taking pride as always with keeping himself nattily dressed when he was free; clean, fresh, and always ready to pick up a request. His obsession had always been to style and dress himself in the best clothes—street gear or otherwise—that money could buy. This *love* still ran deep. Even behind the wall of the prison where he was housed. But his passion clearly was to scam and get money, and to fuck off with many different females.

Physique-wise, this nigga was medium built with an athletic frame. His lips were thick and full, having a slight touch of femininity to them, because they were pinkish, so he'd been told by females he dated.

Always in close space with him face to face, Verena stated one day, "Your eyes, Montell, they're deep and penetrating, you know. Not a bad thing, per se. But not exactly a quality trait either."

"I'm know. And because of this, it causes my facial features and overall appearance to look as if I'm mad at something or in a rage even," he responded. "People don't know how to read me correctly," he further said to her. "And it's common for people to have a strong tendency to misjudge me, due to the *natural gruffly* look I got. But no matter how others view me, I'm content with how I look," he spoke in an emphatic tone of voice. This was a very confident and self-assured man.

Chapter 6

At this point in their acquaintance, he and Verena always found themselves talking quite often while he was at work in her office. The two had yet another in-depth conversation. She was looking to dig deeper into his personal life more. Really deep. She wanted to know the things that his institutional profile didn't have in it. Things he kept close to himself. *I won't know if I don't ask,* Verena thought to herself.

"So, tell me a few more things about yourself, Montell, if you will," she said to initiate the talk this particular morning.

He looked at her and smiled. "Tell you a few more things about me like what?" he responded.

Verena shrugged her shoulders. "I don't know. Whatever you feel like you want me to know. I'm bored. And you and your balance of witty street slang and intelligent way of talking entertain me. You got a good way of how to balance the intelligent you and the thuggish you, I noticed. And so you'll know, I won't judge you. And my office is not a court of law. Anything you say, won't be used against you," she let out. Her humor caused the both of them to share a laugh together. She hadn't done this with a man in over twenty years. Not even with male colleagues.

Montell unleashed. "Check it out then., I'm from Albany. Was raised by momma and step-daddy. I learned at an early age all about real nigga shit. Real nigga protocol. Especially about what it is to be loyal and on the importance of family structure. Momma and Daddy split when I was young, around the age of five. It didn't affect me no kinda way, though. Momma's baby, Daddy's maybe, right," he said with a mischievous smile. "I got one sibling, a sister named Ciara. Me and her pretty close. Both our parents still alive and well. They get along, for the most part, and they carry on a conversation from time-to-time. That's about it though. What else you wanna know?"

He felt like it was something in particular she was getting at. *But what?*

"Maybe about your passions, and your friends. What was y'all like hanging out together, doing what y'all do, you know? Things like that."

He blurted, "Well goddamn! My muthafuckin' profile must be really interesting to yo ass, huh! Or you just nosy as fuck. Which one?" He came back with, smiling, laughing and showing teeth.

"It is. I won't lie," Verena responded.

He immediately responded, "Well look, if this is so, you need to cut the bullshit from here and let a nigga know *exactly* what's on your mind. A'ight. 'Cause I ain't got the time to be sittin' 'round tryna figure things out. Who does that? We too grown for that anyway. So, if you with the shit, then be *all the way* with the shit. You feel me! But if you ain't, you ain't. It can't be no half stepping in the world for you women in nowadays and time, when you wanna know something about a nigga."

"That's understandable. And yes, I will cut the bullshit. In due time, though and on my own terms not yours. I just gotta let things play out like they are and slowly be revealed like they are now too. When I'm completely ready, trust me, you'll be the first to know. But back to what I was originally saying. You and your friends, what was y'all like hanging out together, doing what y'all do? And about your passions?" She gave the best explanation she could possibly come up with and not give in so easily.

"Okay. I gotcha on that. I understand. But anyway, my passions? Shit, scamming! Getting money! Fuckin' different bitches! Being dope boy fresh more than the dope boys be fresh! You know, typical thug-nigga shit. And my niggaz... them... they were few and far in between. Loyalty was a must with us though. Our business dealings were on the up-and-up. Everybody was solid. The connection between me and my niggaz developed when we were attending college together at Georgia State University. We'd gotten attached to one another then, going through the years, and hung out almost daily. When I got to Atlanta, I immediately adopted the *Black Mecca* as my second home. I really fuck with the city. The love me and my niggaz have for one another was surreal. You feeling me?" he worded.

"I do. And I can relate to you on this as well. Me and Tiffany, Mrs. Long, are the same. But me personally, only one friend. No more. And that's Tiffany in there." She pointed towards her secretary's office. "You now know about her being my BFF. No one will ever replace her."

"That's what's up. But with me and my homies, everything was going well, until the day that fuckin' indictment got unsealed, and the government came down hard on our candy asses. Then, all hell broke loose. A fuck-nigga crossed us out when he snitched and became an informant for the federal government. Sucka-ass nigga!" Montell spat vehemently at the thought.

He was pissed now all over again at the memory of what happened.

"Long before I got into white-collar shit, I had always dreamed of going pro to the NBA. I can ball like hell. And I'm one of them niggaz who strongly believe I got a savvy combination of street-sense, book-sense, and yes, common-sense. Maybe this is so. Maybe it ain't. But at all cost I felt the need to test the world to know for certain. The shit I got—supposedly—fixed it to where I had the luxury, to move pass most muthafuckas' of my class. I realized quickly that a profit is far better than a wage any day of the week. I done read and studied books by *Napoleon Hill, Reginald Lewis,* and *Adam Smith,* and others, and these muthafuckas' helped cultivate the ambition and drive I got about myself." Montell went on and on and on in *razzling* and *dazzling* Verena with some of the shit he talked about.

His vocabulary was extensive. He'd learned this when he became a Five Percenter and joined The Nation Of Gods and Earths.

"So, you simply could not force yourself to work a job manually for others, once you discovered that you already had what was necessary, along with the leadership capabilities, to be your own boss, build your own team, and make money your own way, right?" She felt the need to ask.

"Right. And that's a good way to put it," he replied. Confidence and self-assurance oozed. "But I never felt the need to get gangsta' or never took any serious penitentiary chances that carried serious time. By us having motion and moving how we was on a low-key basis, we was able to go unnoticed. We continued in this way, and got rich quick, and never looked back to the days of being broke. *NBA Montell,* is what I myself and my niggaz call me now."

"NBA Montell, you say, huh! And what *exactly* does that stand for?" Her question was asked out of sheer curiosity. She had nothing street about her going on. But always desired to at least be associated with those from this lifestyle.

"NBA is 'Never Broke Again,'" he clarified.

"Always interesting, I see. Always interesting." Verena smiled brightly behind her compliment As they continued talking.

***

"Me and my niggaz had a good run with the things we were doing. This was of course, before the FBI and IRS swarmed in to take us out the game. Shit, we'd cleared roughly $10,000,000 on the streets, before being taken down. The feds discovered all of our shit, and the majority of other money-making schemes that was in play. To add further insult to injury, them muthafuckas' took the laundromats we had, the vending machine services, and other small businesses of ours in and around Atlanta. Other commercial properties was taken, too. The safes where the money was hidden was cleaned out, along with other personal deposit boxes. However, after everything that happened, I *was* smart enough beforehand to see it coming. And I was prepared in my own way," said Montell.

At his mother's advice, Montell set up legitimate businesses in their hometown under her and his stepfather's names. Also, the church his mother was a member of played a part in what he had going on. He stashed a $500,000 nest egg of cash and an additional $500,000 in jewelry in a safe spot at her house. She knew nothing of this.

The money she'd profited from the businesses she operated for him helped him out, too. With this, he was able to pay legal tabs and acquire degrees while in federal lock-up. This was in Constitutional Law and in Economics. And it gave him an advantage in a lot of ways. His future was still bright.

***

Montell had a long conversation with his cellmate one evening. The roommate was an older and more mature dude from Savannah. His name was Harold. They were similar in a lot of ways. And, they had a lot of respect for each other.

"Yo bro, I got a strong determination, to be sure I'm thoroughly ready for the free-world once they let my black-ass go," Montell said. He had plans to take the money and the jewels that was tucked away, and make investments so to build a business of his own, or at least becoming an integral part of a something already established.

"I feel the same way, bro. Ain't nothing to it but to do it, you know. And hopefully, these goddamn parole people gonna let a nigga go sometime soon. It's been long enough. And yeah, I'm qualified to. Just gotta be sure to stand on business once I'm out there again," responded the cellmate. "I ain't got no more room to fuck up."

These thoughts and ideas of theirs were the motivation and the driving force behind the persistent nature they had. Especially Montell, he wanted to succeed at all costs. He simply had to. Failure was not an option for him. Dude was obsessed with his fantasies of becoming a bread winner, but one that was on the right side of the law this go-around.

But at the same time, this would be from the illegal profits he was to scam for to pop things off with. He was on his way to the top again, he felt it, and he felt good about the chances he had. Prison was just a minor setback for a major comeback. Period.

Chapter 7

At a time least expected in his situation, a lucky opportunity came about. Good fortune favors the bold. And since Montell was the one and only inmate who had direct access to an attractive female warden, he was the fortunate one. Being bold was natural for him. In addition, he was confident. He felt he could get her attention and hold her interest exactly like he wanted it. Even more than he already had. *Being rejected isn't something I could afford.* He thought. *I hate the feeling of being snubbed! No nigga likes being turned down. Not even an ugly nigga!*

If there was one thing Montell knew all too well from reading and studying about seduction, it was that the persuasive art form of talking, if utilized the right way—through business, intimacy, or otherwise—could be a validation about the type of man one is, or, to the perception put on display. And now, Montell wanted to find a way to it all.

"There's nothing in the world that can't be negotiated." He reflected on these words quite often.

***

Verena was the type of female who loved sports, and in particular, high school football and basketball. She and Montell had begun to have conversations about this, and he would ask about the progress of those high school teams in and around Atlanta. The ones he knew she kept updated information on.

"Yo, Verena, how is the basketball and football teams you follow doing this year?" He had asked, initiating conversation. A level of comfort was established between them at this point. They both made each other feel down to earth.

"Ah, man, a few of them on a roll, I tell you. *Parkview* and *Greyson* got themselves in stable contention to reach the playoffs on the football field. You know, not long ago, *Greyson* won the state championship. They're great competitors. And the lady basketball teams, is showing a lot of promise and potential as well," she responded. She then switched up to a more serious tone. "And remember: *in private,* I'm *'Verena.'* Around others, I'm *'Ms. Gordon.'* Never forget this, okay?"

"I know that shit! *Dafuq*! It's why I said it," he let out with a laugh. "And oh yeah, that's fantastic. But the high school I went to in my hometown, *Westover High,* got an outstanding record for basketball, both males and females. But, as far as the football teams, I don't know what to make of any football teams in Albany. They don't ever seem to have any success," he stated.

"Hopefully, things will get better in the future," she responded.

The research he'd put in on her, and the knowledge he had of the teams they discussed, gave him the opportunity to dig deeper into the topics and reasons for the successes, failures, challenges, and all other things related. Verena would automatically reply and elaborate with great detail on everything she knew of the teams and the games.

Also, it was many mornings where Montell would ask her for the sports page from the *USA TODAY* newspaper she showed up to work with daily.

"Verena, you already know I gotta have that sports page from your paper once you done, right?" he would say.

"Sure, Montell. No problem."

The both of them would then get into discussions, as she read from the paper and enjoyed her cup of coffee. His duties as her orderly required him to prepare pleasantries for her.

Montell knew exactly how she liked her caffeine infused drink; one creamer, two sugars, and occasionally, a few drops of honey. There were also times he was told to put two spoonfuls of hot chocolate into the brain stimulating liquid. He and his fellow prisoners called these types *"sexy cups."* Verena asked for those mostly on Fridays.

***

Montell would make it his business at every opportunity to initiate further conversation with a question here, *"Verena, you do any reading on your down time?"* And another question there, *"What type of books you into?"*

She would eagerly respond, giving him something insightful, which in return, said a lot about her private life.

"Yes, Montell, I read. And I definitely enjoy it. I think it's mentally and spiritually liberating. I don't really get the opportunity to be the bookworm I once was. I've read so much growing up, to the point that books became my friends, anytime me and Tiffany were not hanging out together. I take from different books though. Most are 'suggested readings' through Oprah's book club and Obama's book club that I'm a member of. Or, some urban fiction material. I've learned that, with these type of books, you can't lose with Wahida Clark, KiKi Swinson, Teri Woods, Loryn Landon, Jazze, Ashley Antoinette, or S. Yvonne Powell, to name a few female authors. And for the men authors, there's Eric Jerome Dickey, Silk White, Cash Alexander, or K'wan, to name a few. I love books by E. Lynn Harris too. And it's a new author who's making a lot of noise of late. Backing it up too, with captivating reads. Actually it's three. A guy by the name S.A. Cosby, and two ladies named Jahquel J and Nia Forrester.

But, if I must say, I tend to prefer books that are centered on uplifting and providing meaningful insight and advice to minorities—females of color particularly—from disenfranchised communities," she had related.

With a response like the one she'd given, it proved to be a clear indication to Montell that, she knew of, understood, and sympathized, with females who deal with struggles and various other issues on a daily basis.

Montell knew from that point, her concerns extended far and deep, in particular, towards females who held no level of power, and primarily, on issues women of color suffer from, rather silently or openly—from love, acceptance, and emotional stability—to the more complex and nationally recognized problems, such as complexion issues, dietary concerns, and ongoing battles with weight or poor health.

Chapter 8

Making Progress...

The mission Montell personally put himself on took roughly two months to complete. He managed to get all he could on the personal life of Verena. He had to thoroughly listen to her too, whenever they talked more, and applying his knowledge on how to *read between the lines.* All that was needed from there was for him to hear her out completely in her own words, and in the way she would phrase things.

Other than his reviews of her social media profiles; *Facebook, IG, Twitter, Plenty of Fish, Bumble, Tender* and *Tag,* Montell made mental notes from up close and personal, and he paid attention to the decor and other items that surrounded her office, along with the ones she would bring to work. And obviously to him now, Verena had no man either. None that he knew of. It didn't take a rocket scientist to figure that out.

Montell talked to his roommate again about Verena, since he'd been there at the prison for years, and was familiar with her more than he was.

"Say, Harold, check this, right? What's your take on the warden bitch I work for, bro? Give it to me raw. And don't hold back nothing. I know you know her better than I do in many ways. You was here when she first got here."

"Nigga, you already know I don't know no other way to give my opinion, Montell. No other way but raw. And you work for her, nigga. You should already know more than me by now." He let out with a chuckle. "All the way 'round the board, you should. But, to be straight up, I think she a thirsty bitch! That hooker is a hopeless romantic. She ain't got no nigga in her life because she don't wanna give up her independence or control she got over niggaz. Not even in a household. I can see straight through her," replied Harold. "And, all y'all tempting ass young niggaz she's surrounded by here, probably makes the bitch cum hard on herself, every time she uses that damn vibrator, I'm sure she got, and have a thought of one of you niggaz. Hell, truth be told, the bitch might be slick choosing you, nigga. She *did* hire yo ass, didn't she? And you the *only* nigga on compound, who's that close to her. Now think about that. And when you finally do catch the bitch, nigga, you better not forget about a nigga either. Because I see it coming. And you got that kinda shit in you to do it." Harold completed his assessment and smiled.

Montell returned a smile of his own of the compliments. "You do got a point. And I had those same thoughts before. But I know she ain't got no nigga in her life, no husband, and no fuck-buddy. Because for example 'bout what I mean, in Mrs. Duncan's office, my counselor, anybody can take notice of all the shit there to prove she got a husband and three kids. She even got pictures of them and the family dog, '*Binky*' included. Mrs. Duncan got a *BEST MOM/BEST WIFE* coffee mug and other shit dotted all 'round her office to prove her status as married. Also, she got the ultimate symbol to show and prove, so to speak. But not this bitch Verena."

"Hell, you able to find out more about her than I can. Again nigga, you *work* for the bitch! So you able to peep everything she's about. Up close and personally."

"Oh, yeah. I agree. But ain't nothing in her office to show a family life in that type of way. Most importantly, like I said, Mrs. Duncan do got the ultimate symbol, one Verena probably only dream of having. My counselor got a big ass diamond ring situated atop her finger. She been happily married for a while now. That, in and of itself, shows the true testament of success about her personal life, being cooperative and easy to live with, for a man to propose to her and ask her hand in marriage," Montell said.

"You been paying attention, ain't you!" Harold came back with, smiling at Montell in amazement. "But from what I see about her, Verena, that bitch is about that shit, my nigga. Real talk! A sneaky bitch always is. And Verena, is a sneaky bitch!"

"Hell yeah, they are. And hell yeah, she is. I done paid attention well enough to know. I got to, in order to get ahead and stay ahead."

"What yo ass up to, Montell?" The veteran chain-gang roommate worded then laughed like crazy.

Montell did the same. They knew one another well from being months long cellies.

They continued on in their locker room style of talking with one another As it got more interesting with each topic.

**

Although Montell was locked up, Verena knew to a certain degree that he was somewhat accomplished in a few ways. In particular, accomplished to the point in being a man of possible interest for her. Any female is persuaded to at least give a man she's around all day, a considerate thought.

The degrees he had become a part of his institutional profile. They were kept by the Department Of Corrections to be maintained and updated regularly. These certificates silently spoke for him.

Montell a smart dude, I see, Verena thought upon going through his profile yet again. With each and every conversation they would have, her interest level raised more and more.

In addition, Verena also knew about the schemes and other operations that Montell and his cohorts had pulled off. She went online and read all about it. The ones that helped them get rich before their incarceration. In all actuality, she became even more curious about him and his hustle and grind mindset and began digging into his personal business indirectly.

Any time a woman does this about a man, it signals that she may be on the verge of giving in, and don't want to regret any decision she makes about doing so moving forward. Maybe this was Verena.

The two were in her office having yet another conversation based on her curiosity and interests in a few things, but most noticeable, him. She was willing to take things a step farther this time though. Way farther.

"Montell, I wanna ask you something again, if that's okay with you?" she mentioned.

"Yeah, wassup, Verena? Again though," he replied with humor. He felt something good coming on, because he sensed she had more personal questions for him today. Not the other way around. "And, you do know that I know that the only time a person who's in a position above someone— you— asks in-depth personal questions to a person who's not on that level—me—is when they've taken interest in that individual personally. Is this you?" This scenario was similar, he felt.

"No. Not *exactly*. And I'm not trying to be in your business or anything like that. But I gotta ask. *How* did you learn that slick-ass way to outsmart the government the way you did? I gotta know. And it's okay to talk candidly with me. I'm a warden and a woman only. Somebody who wants to hear you out. Not another prosecutor or an investigator," she stated and let out a laugh at her own words so to make him feel comfortable.

Montell smiled in delight. He couldn't believe she'd ask him something like this, let alone, so bluntly and in an up close and personal way. Human nature was beginning to take its course, had it not already. He felt privileged to answer her.

"Look Verena, to be honest, that shit really ain't that hard to do. A nigga just gotta be serious about it. Something like I had been. I just brought out my full potential," he responded with absolute confidence.

Verena smiled and became more drawn in behind his well-calculated play of words. His remarks caused her to have a rush of excitement pass through her body. It showed across her face. She even let out a chuckle behind the boldness that this nigga put on display. It was necessary for him to show this indeed, that he was rough around the edges too, and for her not to let all that smart shit fool her about him. Maybe she was testing him to bring out this version of the *street-nigga* or thug-nigga she assumed he was holding back. He was. He had to trust her enough to know that she wouldn't cross him out.

"You make it sound good. But I wanna know is it *ALL* good? That's what I want you to tell me. And of course, in your own way. Now talk," she demanded.

This nigga wasted no time to give Verena what she wanted. "So, you *really* with the shit yourself, ain't you," he said. "I'm hearing it. And hopefully, I could see it too." His roommate's words coming to him now about Verena as he looked at her. "I see now that you 'bout that life too, huh. But I'mma answer you like you want me to. I just need to know if or not, you *not* tryna set a nigga up no kinda way?"

"Nucca! If I wanted to set your ass up, you'd be *set up* already! And why would I do that? You're just one of the most interesting inmates I've had to come through here on my watch. That's all. And I wanna be sure that, I made the right choice in you to be my orderly." *Amongst other things.* "After you wrote to me about the detail, I felt it wasn't no need for me to allow you to sit around in the dorm all day with nothing to do, other than maybe try and find a way to seduce one of my female officers," she stated.

Once I looked you up, I wanted to know what you was all about for myself, Verena thought while eyeing Montell intensely.

The conversation continued for the better part of twenty minutes. He popped his shit on all points relevant to what Verena wanted to know. Rather Montell knew it or not, she was choosing, like Harold mentioned she probably was, and he'd passed the first phase of her process in her endeavor to bring him closer to her personally. And, just like Harold also had said, *the bitch was thirsty!*

Chapter 9

Throughout Montell's years of being locked up, he had read and even studied many books that literally spelled out to a man, how to seduce and persuade women to accept what they have to say or offer. Of course, this is on the basis of the individual man. But, these suggestions could in fact be game theories put to the test. Something women would reason with. Remember, *"if it sounds right, women will reason with it."*

The books he'd buried his mind into was *PIMP: The Story Of My Life* by Iceberg Slim; *From Pimp Stick To Pulpit: Its Magic* by Bishop Don Magic Juan; *Pimpology* by Pimping Ken; and *The Art Of Seduction* by Robert Greene. There were others, but he only felt the need to take from these, per se, since he loved to indulge in the study of seductive culture. He was eager to put those lessons to work.

In the previous conversation he and Verena had, Montell said this. "I want you to realize that, yes, I know exactly what to say and how to communicate it with a lady of your stature. But I had to figure out which way was best with you, so to get you to be willing to compromise your position, and take a chance on fuckin' with me, since you opened the door already for this. Didn't you?"

"Yeah. I did. In a way."

"Okay. And also, I'm looking to find out what you like. Maybe I could deliver it to you. Who knows. I have definitely been known to *deliver*."

THE DIRTY SIDE OF MONEY | PRINCE

"Well, continue to seek. Maybe you'll find," she responded with a smile. "And delivery, is *always* a good thing. *Always* a good thing. Never forget this. Because, if only you knew how happy a woman gets anytime we get surprise deliveries, at our front doors from Amazon or otherwise. We love deliveries."

Dude began to develop a style and a suave way about himself to seduce her spirit to accept him, rather than him do likewise unto her. But it was already there. That thuggish shit was what Verena wanted in her life. He just needed to show more of it. And then, everything would speak for itself. It would come full circle. As the late great Iceberg Slim put it throughout the pages of his book *PIMP, "It's best to be the chosen rather than be the chooser."* Montell learned valuable insight from these lessons.

***

Weeks Later...

Montell paid more attention to the ways and behaviors of Verena. Without a doubt, he had his work cut out for him, as she was no easy task. His boldness really came out this day. The thug-nigga nature of his revealed itself.

"Verena, what will it take for a nigga to get witcha? Be straight up 'bout it."

"I'll try my best to. But seriously, it would take *a lot* of work and *thousands* of dollars even, to have me. I swear to you, Montell, this has to be paid in advance, long before I ever begin taking any chances on losing my job, fucking up my career, or worse, having my goddamn freedom snatched away, for me to deal with someone locked up," she responded.

Verena completely overlooked what Montell's exact question was. He never mentioned anything about an *inmate* having her, per se. He was referring to *any man,* period. She told on herself with her reply. And the crazy part about it was, she didn't even know it.

Ah ha! Gotcha! And once I'm able to convince you that you can believe in me and I could be trusted, and it would be cool to do business with me, if not but so much, yo ass will loosen up and began to give in. You gonna fuck with me. Ain't no doubt in my mind about it, he thought.

With the trust he'd earned to talking as he so fit in conversation, he was able to explain on a deeper level that, "Under no circumstances, Verena, would I put you at risk, if you made the choice to fuck with me. Also, look, Verena," he said. She smiled at him and his bold level of confidence by his continued calling her by her first name and not addressing her by title ever again.

He was allowed to say what he wanted to say and be himself with her fully. "My get money campaign and hustling, didn't stop just because I got locked up. I'm gonna *always* find a way to scheme, scam, and make some bread. Don't get that *shit* twisted! And I'm talking this raw shit with you now, because I feel like I can. It's like you my therapist; every time we talk like this. It's healing for us both, I'm sure. For me, at least, by being able to vent and release. And for you, by being exposed to someone who's *not* from *bougie* society, but actually from the hood. A place you ain't got a clue about." He couldn't help himself. He had to laugh.

She cocked her head sideways and pursed her lips. "True."

"And, I know I'm spitting this real nigga shit your ass really wanna hear me spit. Because if I wasn't, my black ass wouldn't have a damn job with you no more. And I know you get tired of having to be so fuckin' formal all the time on a daily basis."

Her head and lips repeated what they had before. "That's true too."

"But look, if or when you decide to take a chance on *us* getting to know one another more personally, or business-wise, you ain't gotta worry about me jeopardizing you in no type of way. I feel like I know what you want. I can see it, and I sense it. All I ask for is the opportunity to *deliver* to you the shit you might desire. You did say delivery is good, right?"

"I did. But what makes you feel like it's *you* per se, who can do that? Deliver to me what I want?" she asked.

Montell pursed his lips and cocked his head one sided now looking on at her. His smirk was sinister. "Cut the bullshit act you putting on, Verena! I know what I need to know about you, well enough to know what you are searching for and want. Just trust me on that. But like I said, I'm not gonna get you caught up no kinda way. I'll take all the chances. Not you." His choice of words was well placed. They resonated with her.

Verena had everything at her fingertips on what Montell needed. But he wouldn't say right off what. He wanted to be sure she was willing to go the distance. He needed to know if she was in it to win it, WITH HIM, or if she wasn't. *Not* for herself. Also, he needed to further convince her that she would be invisible, if she'd chosen to let them get to know each other differently.

A decision was finally made on her part. "Yes," she said, "we would do business at some point in the near future."

And, not long after, they would begin to get to the money like he suggested. Things was popping off from that point.

Chapter 10

Weeks Later...

The first money-making scheme the two discussed doing was one Montell was all too familiar with and knew how to work well: income tax fraud. During the many days he had the privilege to lounge around in the office with Verena, she would almost always feel the need to ask more questions and have in-depth conversations about the mechanics of how he was able to work the outstanding scams he did. She couldn't help herself.

"Montell, push my door closed a little more and open the blinds wider for me please. I got something I wanna talk with you about today," Verena said.

"It better be worth my goddamn time, too," he responded, and did what she asked him to. He then took a seat in the guest chair. "What's on your mind?" he said, already having an idea of what it was she wanted to talk about.

"So, tell me, without too much elaboration or beating around the bush. Because you never finished telling me before. How did you do it? How in the *hell* were you able to outsmart Uncle Sam at his own damn game? How did you master being a *'crook by the book,'* the way like you did? The reason I ask is because this was started the day you wrote to me and applied for this detail. Not to mention the fact that there are special notes attached to your profile, instructing the warden of each facility you go to, to be sure and keep a watchful eye on you anytime you're around sensitive information. I also got calls from the government the IRS, instructing me to *'watch McNeal!'* I'm gonna let you in on a little something, okay. Although I'm not supposed to do so, I am anyway. I'll make an exception for you. But the feds want detailed reports on you. My boss, the regional director, ordered me to do so. They intend to keep tabs on you and your friends as they do to everybody who *'steals their money,'"* Verena related, with a pinch of sarcasm to her words.

After adjusting in her chair, she continued.

"Your pals have already been cut loose, except one. I don't know if you were aware of this or not," she mentioned.

"I know. I done had a chance to talk to them since they been home," he replied.

"Oh, you have? So, your black ass got a goddamn cellphone back there in the dorm, huh?" she stated with a humorous laugh.

"Yep! You got to know that. All the real niggaz keep a lifeline. I got two of 'em. And?"

"Okay. Don't worry. I'm not gonna have you put in isolation," she replied, overlooking his confession. "But good. Anyway. Part of my report must include who your cellmates are. You and Harold Cummings still in the room together, right?"

"Ah-huh."

"Okay. And also, I have to list your facility phone calls and your visitors. They wanna know who you've been in touch with and for how long, due to you potentially posing a threat to the life of another, so they stated."

"I know this too. That's why I never use the facility phone or get my people to come see me too often. Not even one of my ex-girlfriends, as bad as they want to."

"A Tamron Bryce and a Mandy Barfield, I seen, right?"

"That's right."

"You're a smart guy. But anyway, what happened and how did you do it?" Verena insisted, eager for a detailed answer.

***

Montell went into character and offered to break it down to her with specifics. So much so to the point of a third grader being able to understand what he said. He even took it a step further by explaining *exactly* what happened and who the guilty person was, that caused their downfall.

"Verena, look, if you really wanna know, here it is. This is what happened. One of our guys, a sucka ass nigga named 'Rico, 'caused us to get fucked up This nigga *was* a good friend and partner of ours, before he pulled off the bullshit he did. Anyway, long story short, Rico went out and bought a seventy-thousand-dollar car, a brand-new Mercedes Benz E Class. He paid for it in all cash. This idiot took it upon himself to branch out from what we had going on full time and wanted to try and mix two hustles that didn't coincide with one another. It was as if he tried to mix oil and water by force. Either way you try to do it, it's not gonna happen. Had it not been for the greed on his part, the feds wouldn't have ever launched the type of investigation on us as they had. They set up a sting operation to trap Rico, and that was how he got caught up in the fish net they snagged him with."

Montell paused to look Verena in the eyes for any evidence of astonishment. He then proceeded, "Rico, made it his business to get in the dope game—becoming a heroin dealer. Little did this nigga know, at the time he bought that damn car and paid in excess of ten grand cash, by law, the dealership was required to report the transaction to the federal government, the *IRS* most notably. The fool had his sister co-sign for him, then later turned and placed the car fully under his own name, due to the two of them having a fallout. She was unemployed and so was he, as the businesses he also owned were not under his name either. He made the same foolish move with one of the small businesses as with the car. He didn't get a license and legitimize his transactions."

He took a deep breath and went on. "From that point, the IRS began their investigation. It was discovered; Rico had connections to a large-scale high-level street Kingpin. The *IRS* passed on their findings to the appropriate department, the *DEA* for them to assess the situation. The *DEA* themselves, placed Rico on their watch and were able in capturing him on surveillance. He was around the high-profile supplier they'd long been keeping track of some nigga by the name Jimmy Lawson aka, '*Jimmy Smack,*' who's from Detroit, Michigan. He was an elder founding member of the infamous '*Black Mafia Family*' of that city. The DEA then set up a sting operation to nab Rico, in the hopes he would rat, then lead them to Jimmy Smack, by revealing all he knew of the guy—how he moved, and what ties to his operations he could loosen for them with information. That fuckin' snitch-bitch Rico, did just that! He ratted out Jimmy smack! But in addition to blabbering on Jimmy and seriously violating the G-Code, that fuck-nigga told on *us* too in the process. For no reason! What part of the fucking game was that?"

"Wow! Some nerve with that guy, huh! What was that nucca thinking?"

"Fuckin' right, it was! And I don't know what the fuck that nigga was thinking. But anyway..."

Verena was giving Montell her full attention as he related the past. She wanted to know everything. Not that she didn't already. Just checking once more to know how real he could be.

He kept going "But, it was Rico, who'd messed up and sold a half a kilo of dope to an undercover agent in a hand-to-hand exchange. The shit was caught on camera. He'd gotten arrested an hour after the sale went down. To avoid an extended stay in prison, he gave a treasure trove of information to the DEA and IRS on all the activities we had going on. This pussy-nigga essentially exposed the everything of *our* day-to-day operations! Had it not been for him snitching to save his own ass and prevent himself from feeling the burn of the punishment that awaited him in court behind the bullshit from his own actions, and if he had kept to the script by telling only what the feds wanted to know about '*Jimmy Smack,*' our crew would've been well between the fifteen to twenty-five million dollar bracket by now and living good in the free world. But noooo! Rico contributed to us getting knocked off! Everybody on the team went down—Me, Jamie Hamilton, Eric Mickens, Roderick Grady, and of course, Rico Locus. We called ourselves '*The Black Hand,*' because it was five of us. You have to excuse my French on this one too, Verena."

"Speak your mind. You got the leeway to do so."

"To be real with you, all of our *dicks* got thrown in the dirt because of this bitch-ass nigga Rico! He fucked all of us over!"

"I see!" Her facial expression didn't change much. She was genuinely interested in what he was saying, so he finished.

"We all got average sentences to serve in the feds *by the guidelines* for what we'd done. Everybody but Rico. I was the only one to get hit with additional state time, once the federal part was over. That's how I ended up here. Rico, on the other hand, got a separate sentence from the one all of us went down on. The judge gave him eight years for the sell of narcotics to the agent. Although he cooperated, he was still sentenced to serve a longer stretch than he was first under the impression he would get from the judge. The coward entered into the *Witness Protection Program* as soon as he got into the system, to avoid having a contract put out on his life by Jimmy Smack's people, since Rico testified in the jury trial the guy had. Rico, chose to do all of his time on

'*PC,*' unless he later decided to sign off at some point."
Montell related to Verena the entire story without her so
much as interrupting at any time. It clearly let him know she
was committed to hearing him out.

"I'mma be real with you about something, Verena?"

"Absolutely, Montell. Feel free. You already have been
for the most part, I assume. And so you'll know, keep in
mind that anytime we're alone like this, it's absolutely okay
for you to continue calling me Verena. I'm cool with it. Since
you already done made it your business to man up in this
way anyway. But DO NOT EVER fuck up nucca and utter
my goddamn name around nobody else," she said with a
smile and a chuckle. "Don't *ever* fuck up and say my name
around *nobody* else like you do in here with me. Okay."

"I know that shit too! *Dafuq* you mean! Ha! But that's
understandable. And like I already said, I feel like you're my
therapist and we having a session anytime we get into it like
this. But I really hope that that pussy-ass nigga Rico, gets all
the fuck he deserves while in prison, long before his
scheduled release date. That nigga deserves to die! And
should! That's the true hope I got for a '*friend*' who turned
enemy when he snitched," Montell emphatically stated. "All
fuckin' rats must die!" He added to further express his
deepest feelings towards the guy.

The conversation the two held lasted maybe ten minutes
longer. Montell was able to school her on a few things related
to taxes, about the ins and outs of preparing tax forms online,
and several other key points related to the hustle. Basically,
things she'd already known but hadn't known how crooks
made it work for them. All of this occurred before he left her
office, in addition to the story of he and his friends' arrests.

Chapter 11

It was a known fact by Montell and the others that Rico lied to the feds on his friends and over-exaggerated many things in the process. He thought that his lies would be the determining factors to get him off the hook, or that he would qualify for a reduced sentence. His attempts for a lenient punishment failed, due to the judge not accepting his, *"I've made mistakes,"* apology to the court. He ended up being sent to the prison system anyway, to serve the time originally imposed. His *"Motion for Sentence Reduction"* had been flat out *DENIED!*

The reality Rico feared most, was the fact that he could be killed just as easily in prison as he could on the street, by any of the hired hitters Jimmy Smack issued the contract to.

"Y'all gotta be sure to protect me while I'm inside," Rico pleaded to the Assistant United States Attorney who prosecuted his case. *"I fear for my life being endangered. I wanna request Protective Custody, right here, right now! That dude Jimmy Smack got connections everywhere! He could possibly have somebody try to kill me!"*

Rico's fears were serious. Basically, Rico had the guilt of a snitch. The psychological impact that weighed heavily on his mind had turned him into a paranoid-schizophrenic. He seemed to always be in a state of panic. Most of the time he served, he was in the confines of protective custody and locked in his cell twenty-three hours a day, sometimes twenty-four at his discretion. Dude was scared as shit.

The information Rico provided to the government, along with his in-court testimony, aided in having Jimmy Smack's ass being handed to him in the form of a *"life sentence."* Rico's anxiety levels ran high and near overheated behind his guilty conscious.

No doubt, a hit was put out on the life of Rico, if only the killers were able to get to him. The BOP wasn't going to be able to shield him for the remainder of all his days of living. To frankly speak, this bitch-ass nigga had to get it one way or another! Montell and the others felt, as they could hardly wait until the day that they got word he had been murdered, either by Jimmy Smack's people, or by some other way, possibly by the dudes that Montell himself had put on the mission to kill his ass. He'd put a hit out too.

***

Presently...
Montell's last standing *true* comrades was living well again the other three. As expected, they got back to handling their business and getting to the money, doing white collar schemes, swiping and scamming and the whole nine yards. They'd reunited and laid a new foundation from scratch. With their mission now being to get it from the ground up and avoid getting arrested again, Montell was the missing link.

They utilized their networking skills to forge ties with foreigners and others while inside. These new connections wanted to do business through their liquor stores, check cashing joints, credit unions, and other financial satellite centers. They were vouched for. These spots were located in Atlanta, New York, Miami, and the Philadelphia areas. Elsewhere too. Roderick was from Philly, so this worked out well for him in his city.

They were fortunate to get things flowing again, long before Montell was to be resurrected and then, they would await his decision to either get on board, or turn down the offer. His choice. Talking about facing peer pressure in the near future. He was definitely set to go up against this.

But in addition, Montell had also befriended the brother of a Colombian drug lord. Maybe he would explore this option too, dealing dope and scamming. Who knows. But this was the same shit he criticized Rico for doing. Hypocritical tendencies always had a way of taking affect in others who was once close to a hypocrite themselves. Montell needed to tread lightly.

Eric, on the other hand, with the knowledge and intellect that this nigga had, he was the one mostly responsible for the come up the freed trio already was experiencing. He was *That Nigga!*

Montell said to him on an occasion not long ago, "Yo E, if no one hadn't known any different, they'd think that yo sly, waffle-colored ass, had stashed money away for hard times long before we got locked up, my nigga. The same as I had done. And you probably had more than me stashed." Montell had basically asked a question indirectly.

"Nigga, you know I did! How you think I was able to bounce back so strong? So, yeah, I was sure to put up some bread," he replied.

To Eric's credit, he was a very brilliant dude, no doubt.

In the past, Eric once told them all to their faces, *"I'mma always be on top of you niggaz and the silent leader of this crew of ours here,"* he emphatically stated. *"I'm smarter than y'all niggaz. It'll never be no point in time where you niggaz will out do me at anything! Never!"* He meant all that he'd said. And with passion, too. He took his own words to heart.

Eric had always felt he was this immaculate and extraordinary type of dude, who the others were beneath. His lighter complexion of skin added to the vehement level of arrogance he had. These kind of dudes could potentially be a handful to deal with. They got cutthroat tendencies.

***

Just like his comrades, Montell himself, was afforded the opportunity to meet a few high-profile dudes throughout his prison sentence in federal lock up. All of this would play a part in his second coming once he gets out, something like that of Jesus Christ, The Messiah. The one guy in particular who stood out more so than most, was the infamous Bernie Madoff, federal inmate number 61727-054.

"Me and Bernie turned out to be good buddies," Montell related to Verena.

"Oh, y'all was? And this probably why the goddamn government seems to wanna keep tabs on your black ass like they do! It's because of your acquaintance to Bernie *fucking* Madoff, Maurice! They ain't through with him yet. They still discovering things this man did. And they certainly ain't through with your ass either, nucca! Not from what I can see," she said.

Montell's first stop had been at *FCI-Butner,* in Butner, North Carolina, the facility where Mr. Madoff was housed.

"That might be true. But Bernie was a really cool and affable individual. He was someone I gained much respect for, opposite all the negativity that the government managed to spew all over the man's name and reputation."

"You just need to keep this in mind and be careful, okay. That's all you need to do. Because that man, Bernie fuckin' Madoff had executed the largest Ponzi scheme in history, defrauding thousands of investors out of an estimated $65 billion over the course of at least 17 years! And some say it may have been in operation as early as the 1960s! According to what I'm reading here. So again, you're guilty by association, nucca. And you need to be careful. Tread lightly, okay. Tread lightly."

"No doubt. But anyway, as you may know, Bernie was also a pioneer in electronic trading and chairman of the

Nasdaq stock exchange in the early 1990's. Bernie took the time out from his day to teach *me*—another nigga who so happen to be in prison right alongside him—the many ins, outs, and how to work the complicated aspects of how the stock market really functioned. He also taught me how to properly and wisely invest so as to maximize the return of profits. He explained about the companies he felt best to buy into, which ones held the potential to perform well, and certainly, the ones to 'stay the hell away from,' in his words. I learned many valuable lessons about business and on life from Mr. Madoff, and I'm gonna forever be grateful and blessed for having the benefit of him as a friend," declared Montell.

"Again, you just be careful, nucca! That's all you do, Mr. *Good Buddy* of Bernard fuckin' Madoff!"

"I will."

Bernie linked Montell with a few older shrewd investors up in New York City. Montell had plans to connect with them once he was free and move on up in the world of money. He would always salute Mr. Bernard Madoff, at every opportunity he had, for simply being a really good guy.

Chapter 12

A few days passed after the time Montell and Verena had the opportunity to be all alone in her office once more and have another heart-to-heart discussion on different topics. They were back at it, yet again, in the privacy of her office, having another chat on the same subject. Things had gotten really interesting this time around. She firmly and unequivocally pointed out exactly what her position would be, *if or when* she made the *"decision to do business"* with him.

Verena was very discreet in how she made her interests known, and that was for very good reasons. Montell had to pick up on her words and know what she was talking about through the riddles she made. It was easy.

He took careful notice to everything she'd said from that point forward. The riddles began to go away.

"I'mma be straight up with you, Montell," she began. "Once I feel that a bond has been seriously built with you, I'll finally reveal all I truly desire and strive to have in life. But on the opposite side of things, you gotta find a way to be sure I too, understand all that you will and will not go for, at the point of us getting the ball rolling. Okay, I'm just putting you up on game in how I want you to deal with me."

Indeed, there was a huge risk factor on his end as well. One that had to be kept in mind. Any level of progress would be carried out with a bit of caution, and he had to walk lightly, since she was a state official, and had tremendous pull within her position. They both communicated this to one another. She went first.

"But, if you wanted to know what I desire and strive to have in life, I'mma share some of it with you right now. You think you can handle it?"

"What kinda question is that for a nigga of my caliber! *Dafuq*! Can *you* handle telling me this shit? That's the million-dollar question. But go ahead. I wanna know what in the world it is that you Verena Gordon want out of life. Pop yo shit."

She couldn't help but smile. "Truthfully, I want a solid man in my life."

"Don't all y'all *bougie* bitches want the same," he came back with quickly.

"No-you-didn't, nucca." She let out, now wildly smiling more and feeling relaxed to continue down this line of conversation. It's always been about him for her. Not her for him. This was different for a change.

"But talk to me. Let your hair down and pull up your skirt more for me. In other words, I want you to get as comfortable as possible while you talk to me about *you*."

"Oh, you do? Is that what you want?"

"Muthafuckin' right,it's what I want. You can trust me. Because now, I'mma be *yo* therapist for today. Or maybe your male companion even. But keep talking, and I'mma keep listening."

"Gotcha! But anyway. I want a solid, hardcore type of dude in my life now, like I had back in high school. That boy knows he really rocked my world! He used to fuck me like crazy. And he had good dick. Even to this day, I still know what it feels like to have him inside of me. But, in addition to wanting a solid guy in my life again, I do at least want one child. And I wanna know what life is like to be *regular.* I never really had that opportunity. I'm the only one my parents had, as you know. And I was groomed and prepared to be who I am. I never had to struggle. I don't know anything about what regular women of color has to go through daily. And I try to tune in and take from the experiences of the Black women who work here at the prison under me and who talk with me. But again, I don't know how to relate to them, and they don't know how to take me. I guess this is because I was spoiled rotten. Or maybe because I was sheltered by my parents. I went to an all-girls Christian school until I started college. And finally, I had myself a taste of freedom. I just wanna be a good wife and an even better businesswoman. If this makes sense?" Her confession was real.

"It do. And I must be the goddamn Pope of Rome now, with all that fuckin' confessing you just made. Whatever you do, don't ever tell on yourself. But I can tell that your momma and daddy protected yo ass from the *real world* and niggaz like me and that nigga you had in high school. Because it was too many hard dick niggaz out there for you at the time," he said with a laugh. "And now, you're exploring. But to be real with you, I feel like, *I'm* the nigga, that can get your stuck-up ass right!"

Verena let out a loud burst of laughter herself. "So, I'm stuck-up now, huh?"

"You already know that shit! *Ha!* I ain't gotta tell you about you," he expressed. "And I'm sure you got book smarts. It's evident. I bet you could kill a differential equation exam. And maybe all else in a technical sense. But I'm willing to bet too, that the nigga you was fucked up 'bout back then, had plenty of street smarts. And book smarts will never be better than street smarts after five P.M. This had to be his advantage over you and why he appealed to you in the way that he did. He was street smart. That nigga probably ran circles around your ass, didn't he?"

"You're right. I am. I could. He did. It won't. It has. And again, he did. He definitely did that. ..ran circles around my gullible ass. And I've been told that many times. But, you may be right. And, you may be heading in the right direction with things. Besides, you're almost a free man. And, there's nothing that'll be holding you back once you get out. No probation. No parole. Not from what you say and from what I've seen."

"Yeah, I know. But yo ass is a little *too* stuck-up for me currently. You need to loosen up more. And try not to be so goddamn controlling and formal with everything! It ain't necessary. Damn! You gotta develop a down-to-earth type of mindset and personality. It's like you too damn programmed, shawdy!"

They both laughed at his words about her.

Montell was able to make it make sense to Verena. This was something she needed. Somebody to tell her ass straight. It was too much like she was a fucking high class white woman who was trapped in a fine ass black woman's body. She was completely out of touch with her ethnicity in general, and the Black community as a whole. But, as Montell said, he felt like he was the nigga, who would get her stuck up ass right. In due time, he'd know.

Chapter 13

Another major step that had to be taken on Montell's behalf was that he needed to thoroughly let Verena know in strong terms, and in the best way possible, certain things he felt she needed to know.

"Look, Verena. Once we get this shit poppin' with establishing business together, it won't be no more such thing as you—the *warden*—instructing me—yo orderly—to do certain shit no more, or to perform certain tasks in that way. In my view, it would then be, *I know something about you, and you know something about me.* That type of vibe. In other words, the both of us would be forced by association to comply with the wishes of each other. Whether we want to or not. And it may be certain demands included in this as well. Just so you'll know, sweetheart."

"I'm aware you're a man, Montell. And I won't be trying to order you around no more like you a flunky or something, working for me in prison," She replied. What was understood didn't need to be explained.

One of the main questions in Montell's mind about Verena, turned out to be a somewhat complex one to understand on his own accord, since he had no knowledge or insight of her aim or intentions. He didn't know if she was trying to set him up and have him condemned to do more time in prison or what.

And so, he needed to first find out if she was being for real with him in her designs to get money or not. After all, she *was* the person to tell him that the federal government wanted *her* to keep tabs on him and turn in detailed quarterly reports of his stay at the prison. So, he had good reason to move in the way things required him to move with caution.

Montell also silently questioned whether this *preppy and bougie bitch,* really wanted to get money and be rich and make her dreams come true, or if she only wanted to continue at thumbing through glam magazines and remain stuck in front of a TV screen *Keeping Up with The Kardashians* and wishing she was one of them? The answers to the questions in his mind had begun to be revealed slowly but surely through her.

"I'm the type of woman Montell, who's all about showing and proving at any available opportunity that I have. I'm very calculated and meticulous in *all* that I personally do or agree to do in business," she declared. He couldn't believe his ears at the words she'd spoken unto him. He was shocked.

Before long, Verena became more serious with her looks and her demeanor when they spoke about real life shit. She'd began taking on a different outward impression, after the last in depth talk they had. Whether they wanted to acknowledge it or not, they were putting a game plan into motion. Montell just needed to see it through.

***

Meanwhile...

In the aftermath of the killing of Keno by Eric and Nasha, and them having the body to make disappear, they finally had a chance to talk and she having to tell him about everything. They were seated in her living room, the site of the crime scene. Nasha's daughter was off at school on this afternoon. So, the level of privacy was established.

Eric started in on the subject by asking, "Nasha, take me all the way back on everything. To the very day you got suspicious and began to find out what you did about dude molesting Zakeya," he said. He wanted a clear explanation from her.

"Bruh, this shit started about a month before the day I confronted the nigga about it," she responded. Nasha was animated in body language and punctuated with her words. She could be extra at times. She had the looks and attitude that would put you in the mind of Akbar V., the aggressive girl from the reality TV show *Love and Hip-Hop Atlanta*. The two had a lot of similarities about themselves.

"That far back?"

"Hell yeah. Beginning the day I took notice that Zakeya hadn't used any of the tampons that I had in the bathroom for both of us to use. I know the little bitch's cycle better than she do. But she ain't use any for the month, which meant something wasn't right. Something was off. So, this immediately let me know she was hiding something, because we have our periods around the same time. This shit made me get suspicious. I went to her room one day while she was at school and started snooping around. Little girls are real careless at hiding shit. Especially when panicking. I know. I used to be one myself. So, I make it to the closest and begin going through things in there. How 'bout, I mess around and stumble up on a fucking pregnancy test that was wrapped in saran wrap outta my kitchen! It was inside the pants pocket of a pair jeans of hers pushed to the back of the closet."

"What! So, she was intending to hide her pregnancy from you to begin with?"

"Apparently so. This probably was because I had once told the little bitch that, if she ever got pregnant before graduating and being grown enough to go on her own and be in her own place, that I would beat her so bad, that the baby would die, and she would wanna die herself, to stop me from beating her ass some more!"

"So, you put the fear of God in her, huh."

"The fear of *ME* first, nigga, and God's ass next! *Dafuq* you mean," said Nasha, adding a sense of humor to the equation.

"But what you do when you took notice of these two things, her missing her period and you finding the pregnancy test?"

"I know I couldn't just ask her lil hot-ass straight up what the deal was, because she would've lied flat out from being scared of what I said I would do. And that would've pissed me off even more. So, I put myself back into the mind frame of a fourteen-year-old girl to think on what I would do to hide something like that from momma. Zakeya always comes straight home from school like I told her to, so she could clean up and get things in place for me to come home from work and take over. And she fucking now. So, I know she wasn't sneaking out the house at night or wasn't going to some lil' boy's house after school. So, I came to the conclusion that she had to be either fucking at school or skipping school to go get laid. I then went to the school myself to kinda sneak up on her and to check to know what her attendance was. How 'bout, the lil bitch had been cuttin' school at least two days out the week for almost two months. Plus, around the time when I got suspicious, me and Keno had been fucking one evening, and I happened to catch a whiff of Zakeya's favorite perfume coming off his ass. She loves *Curve Crush* for women. And this was one of them days that I had him to take her to the eye doctor for her exam and new glasses."

"Oh shit! I know your mind really went to work then, huh."

"Yes *dafuq* it did! I immediately stopped fucking his ass, right then and there. I never said what was up. Because I really didn't wanna believe what my senses had revealed to me. And then, I went to thinking back to the times I needed Keno to go with Zakeya to the dentist to have her braces tightened and to take her to Office Max for school supplies, and to make other runs with her I wasn't able to make. He was paying for everything anyway, so. And then,the shit hit me. Hit me so hard, like it was a goddamn freight train at a hunnid miles an hour coming down the track, bruh."

"Damn! I can only imagine. But the fragrance of her perfume on his..."

"On his neck and chest!"

"On his fuckin' neck and chest, sis! Geeze! That shit was just too much of a fuckin' coincidence for you to over look, I bet!"

"Right. And I put two-and-two together, and then, connected all the dots and had a clear picture on what the fuck was really going on."

"It wasn't no way you could've told yourself that this wasn't so, when in fact, you had everything there in front of you to say that *'it was so.'*"

"Right. So, I found my way to a technology shop that sold mini cameras and shit. I also had the white guy who owned the shop to explain to me how to activate the cameras on the smart TVs we got and link everything to my phone. He did this too. So, I installed the cameras during the time when Keno took a trip to Texas. He and his brothers. I knew he was gonna be gone a couple days, so I had time to do what I do. And then, the truth finally came out. This nigga was fucking my daughter. I knew Zakeya had another doctor's appointment coming up for her sinuses. So I had Keno to take her."

"You laid a trap for his ass?" "Yep! I set his ass right up. He ain't know a thing."

"And what else happened?"

"I saw everything, bruh. Everything that was there for me to see. This was two days before I confronted him about it and shot his ass."

"So, this was long after you found the pregnancy test?"

"Yeah. Long after. And on the day that I confronted him, I sent Zakeya away to momma's house for the weekend. It was just me and that nigga in the house. I played it smoothly too. Had fucked the nigga and everything, to make it seem like nothing was wrong."

"So that's why he was naked in the bed when I pulled up?"

"Mm-hmm. That's exactly why."

"But go ahead. Tell me the rest."

"Once I fucked him good and he was on the verge of going to sleep, I then drew down on the nigga with the gun that he bought me. I showed him the videos I had. It was two of them. Back-to-back days. He couldn't lie. There was no way to do that. He got so mad at me, and we argued like all hell in the moment. The nigga then was about to get up out the bed and rush over to the closest to get his gun to shoot me, but I popped his ass then and there where he laid."

"You ain't did nothing wrong, sis. That was what you was supposed to have done, pop that nigga ass just like you did. And for any nigga who take it upon themselves to rape and molest lil girls—any females for that matter—them niggaz deserve to die to! Real talk! But I wanna know something else. How did you confront Zakeya about everything?" "I just went to her straight up like a mother supposed to. But I never mentioned anything about Keno to her. This was after we got rid of him. I pushed up on her and showed her what I found in her room. I had a new one too, so I could test her there on the spot if she was to lie and say the one I found was somebody else's. She didn't. She said it was her's and that she's pregnant. But was terrified like all hell to say anything to me about it."

"Shit, could you blame her," he remarked with a chuckle.

"Nah I couldn't. But I did give her an ear full though and told her that she was *definitely* gonna have an abortion, which I eventually made her have not long ago. And that's what I did. I made her an appointment to have that damn baby terminated."

"Did you make her tell you who she was pregnant by?"

"No. I never asked anything on those lines and she never said anything along them either. I just let her think that her little secret was safe all to herself. But I did mention to her that Keno and I had broken up for good this time. That he wouldn't be coming back to our house ever again."

"Oh, okay. I was wondering how you managed to dress that up."

"Yeah. I *definitely* dotted all my Is and was sure to cross all my Ts. So, we good on that."

"That's what's up. But in the meantime, I'mma need you to get ready to move away to a different spot for the time being. Maybe for a year or so. Probably up in Marietta somewhere, at least until everything blows over good. And I was sure to burn that mattress and the blanket and sheets and shit too. We couldn't afford to leave nothing behind that had that nigga's DNA on it. But what about his people? They buying the story you sold them?"

"So far, yeah. For the most part. They did push up on me twice about him though. I made fake tears come up in my eyes and played like I was emotional about the nigga. But the belief with them now is that he may had went out to serve somebody some product somewhere, was kidnapped, robbed, and killed. This happens all the time in the city."

"Tell me about it. Did they report anything about a missing person to the police?"

"Not to my knowledge. We should be good. But yeah, I think it'll be a good idea to move away for the time being too. And I did keep all the money he had stashed at the house. So, we good on that too. It was $600,000."

"Bet. Y'all should be straight for a little while then."

"Yeah, we should."

The conversation didn't last too much longer between the siblings on the same subject. Eric had business he needed to go handle with Jamie, and Roderick. And Nasha, needed to get busy in search of a new house to live. All was well and ended well. The situation had gotten handled in the way they saw best and then thoroughly covered up. A job well done.

***

Meantime...

Of all the days Montell had been around Verena and of service to her, he had never had the type of treatment like the one she had begun to give him once he'd elaborated on the details of how his scam worked. Her position on things basically came down to whose side was she on? Was she still with that of the state, or with that of getting money with him?

Verena's intentions shifted. She had a different point of view now. She appeared to be more on Montell's side than she was with the government. Again, it *appeared* this way. The smoke hadn't settled just yet.

On this one particular day, when he had been busy dusting down things and tidying up her office, she told him once again to push her door closed far enough, because there was something she wanted to tell him. Her approach was bolder on this day. She didn't beat around the bush and got directly to the point.

"Montell, listen to me carefully, okay. And you listen good. But before I go into what I really want to talk about, let me say this much. You're a brilliant and fascinating guy in many ways. You got a lot going for yourself, and you got a bright future ahead of you, if you continue to keep your head on straight, humble yourself a little more, and discover how much better off you can become, if you eliminate the many friends you have."

He had already let her know that it was one of their *friends* who had them nailed, and she knew that the possibility existed it could be his "friends" to cause another downfall. Verena continued, "Keep your business really close to no one but yourself, and find ways to get better at blending in, instead of '*standing out,*' as you have a tendency to do at times. If you're capable of balancing this, then I can promise you, a world of opportunity will open up for you to fully explore," she stated.

"I thank you and I truly appreciate your words of counsel and advice. I'll be sure to take heed to it all," he responded. "Now pop yo shit you wanted to pop."

She then went on with what she wanted to say to him. "Now that I've gotten that part out the way, hear me on this. If one iota or even an fuckin' syllable of what I say gets back to me of anything we talk about from this point moving forward, I promise you nucca, and may God be my witness, I'll place something so drastic and devastating on you and in your profile, to where twenty to forty more years of time will be added to the time you're serving now! And not only that, I'll see to it that you serve it on high max security, in a lock-down unit in *Jackson State Prison!* You got that?" She emphatically stated while staring him down menacingly with those deadly piercing eyes of hers and stabbing at him through the air with her ink pen.

Montell stood in confusion, trying to read between the lines and understand the message she was conveying. Finally, he got it and gave in to her in a submissive type of way. "I gotcha. I totally understand." A serious rush of energy detonated inside of him, because he knew his *mojo* and savvy output had worked.

She then continued. "Let's say this for starters, if I considered so-and-so about any business with you... x... y... or z... what all would you need, to make *me* a rich woman. . . mastermind? How is it that you could help *me* become a millionaire, as I've read in your profile you had once became?" she asked of him in a direct way.

Dude looked squarely into this bitch's eyes, squinted, as his eyes met hers, then attempted to try and read her thoughts, as they seemed to come across her forehead. They read; *who wants to be a millionaire? Me—Verena Evette Gordon does—that's who!*

He responded, "Question, is this you finally telling me what your true ambitions is? And I don't want to hear too much of anything about the bullshit you done already said to me you wanted in life, Verena. Give me the raw shit. The real you," he stated.

Verena really wanted to be a richer woman. She was money-hungry to death. She desired to be well off, and, in control while being so. This was her reply.

"Say for instance, Montell, if one person wanted to be a millionaire, and had access to another person that actually was one, what would the non-millionaire need to put into progress, in order to make themselves equal to the millionaire friend of theirs?" she asked.

"Technically, they would want to begin by establishing a partnership, a business bond, and a rapport with them. They would also say and do all that's necessary, to gain the interest of the millionaire friend, in order to have them teach their tricks of the trade, the things that would elevate them to being a millionaire as well," he related. He knew where they was going with this. He was ready. Ready as never before.

Chapter 14

Since Verena had around her an inmate who had some level of experience at being in the $1,000,000 and above bracket, she felt it necessary to explore her options by *politicking* her way through to getting him to agree to a few things. The gesture itself let Montell know that she was for real, based on the fact that she issued a serious threat beforehand without so much as cracking a smile in doing so. She didn't produce any nonchalant energy either. This became scary for him in a way.

In his answer to the question asked, he was demanded to elaborate. He broke things down for her.

"Look, Verena, in all actuality, everything *we* need, you literally got at your fingertips," he stated.

"How so?"

"Shit, all you gotta do is, give me the green light to do the work I know best how to do. And then, I'm all in on it. I can make it pop from there."

"Is that right."

"You better know it!"

"Share more."

"Will do. So, I don't know if you know this or not, but, of the twelve-hundred or so inmates here at Phillips State Prison, at least five-hundred or so, could be utilized in the scheme without a single soul knowing a goddamn thing. It's easier than you may imagine," dude stated.

"Montell, if anything, what do *I* have at risk? Tell me that?" she questioned behind his scamming preamble.

"Not a goddamn muthafuckin' thing, sweetheart! You ain't got shit to worry about. Scared money don't make no money, ya dig! And the only thing you got to fear, is fear itself! Now quit playing with me, Verena, and let's get this fuckin' bread off these other niggaz information, *shawdy,* before somebody else do! You hear me." Montell exhibited a solid level of confidence and persistence in his delivery.

Since Verena didn't have any knowledge whatsoever on anything related to *white collar* or *corporate* scams, she was completely baffled by his remark. "Give me more, Montell. You got to give me more," she demanded, then used her hand to fan back and forth in gesture for emphasis.

Montell gave her what she'd asked, "Verena, we now live in the '*information super age,*' and the personal information of unbeknownst inmates, could become of value to us, if properly utilized. Our bank accounts and pockets could potentially be flooded with money like no other," he stressed.

His aim and intention was to sell her a dream. He wanted to construct 'diamond clustered mansions' in her mind with the eloquence of speech. A good talk game was always known to work magic on the ears and on the heart. And in some cases, the spirit included. The serpent that whispered to Eve for her to finesse Adam out of his position, was a smooth talker too. Again, *there's nothing in the world that can't be negotiated.*

Montell had to completely convince Verena to go for all he had to say or suggest to her. Even if that meant to over-exaggerate things by adding a little more than necessary. By all means this shit had to be done.

Her eyes widened. She sat perfectly still in her seat. She went over in her mind the possibilities of instantly becoming richer.

She then let out, "If that be the case like you just said, then, I want a part of it. I'm in. You got me," she declared. "You just be careful and not get us fucked up, nucca! Because just the sure, if it came down to it, I'll put *everything* all on your ass, Mr. *friend* of the ponzi scheme master, Bernie fuckin' Madoff! He's the one who taught you what you now know." She muttered like she'd already been arrested and in the interrogation room being drilled by investigators.

Montell laughed off her remark and made it his business to talk the best game possible and utilize the most preposterously of inflated terms he could muster up. He had her undivided attention now, so it was a must to go as hard as he could and at full throttle the way he did.

***

As this nigga spit his game and played to her greed, he found a way to assure Verena yet again, that, "Any role you was to play, you would be completely invisible. And absolutely no one would know anything of your involvement. You would be a *ghost,* so to speak. One who would reap the fruit of our labor. Now stop being so goddamn scared, won't you, Verena! This shit too easy."

She smiled at him. Her expression was a pleasant one. He was given reason to believe she was on board. Besides, she said she was. Everything he'd said had worked, and a verbal contract of commitment was had. She was now locked in with the scamming thug that he was.

***

A little more explanation was provided to really seal the deal and have her crazy interested. He felt there could be no room for her to contemplate whether or not she would be making the wrong decision.

"Verena, look, all you have to do is, go to the medical files of the inmates on your computer there," he pointed with a forefinger to the monitor atop her desk, "and print out a specific list of niggaz whose ages range from twenty to twenty-nine maybe, up to thirty-five even. Then, from there, I'll be able to get the show on the road. Like I said, if you go to the medical files of the potential *'clients'* we might be able to use, you'll be able to get their full names, their dates of birth, and their social security numbers, to completely fulfill the requirements of the documents that are gonna be used. And once I got the printouts and my people and I do our part with the other shit, it won't be a problem at all to have the claims returned and collect the money. My niggaz on the street, got a list of *'Employer Identification Numbers'* to many top paying companies that we will be able to register our *'clients'* under as *'employees.'* Also, we'll be able to create our own shell corporation in the long run and incorporate, *'for income tax purposes.'* All of the claims we gonna submit would be for no less than five thousand for each person. Of course, that means our *clients* here I'm speaking of. So, if you do the math, five thousand times five-hundred, what's the return?" he asked and paused for her to give him an answer.

Verena unlocked her cellphone, hit the icon for the calculator, then rapidly punched in the numbers he'd empowered her with. Her eyes became starlit gazes at the numbers she calculated. She licked her lips to taste the sweet savor of success that lay directly in her reach. This would be such easy money.

In astonishment, Verena spoke up to make him aware of the math she had computed. "Maurice! That's two point five million dollars," she let out.

He waited to let the effect of such a big number resonant within her before he offered a reply. "Duh! I know that shit." A smile came across his face.

Verena then dug in deeper for more, "How long you and your boys been up to no good, making this type of money?" she asked.

"Me and my niggaz, you meant to say. And Verena, shit, again, you done read my profile already. You probably know more about me in that way than I do," he teased. "There's something you must also keep in mind," he added.

"And what might that be?"

"This shit is *not* a guaranteed thing, okay. Let's get that understood. It's *only* a hustle, okay. Nothing more. It's only a hustle. But might I have you know that the success rate on returns are anywhere between eighty-five to ninety percent, in the way that my people and I prepare them. The IRS can't tell the difference between the '*real*' McCoys and the '*fake*' McCoy's," he said to persuade her more.

She continued to sit and remain silent, simply staring at him in amazement beyond natural observation. "And exactly how do you and *your* team go about actually getting the money?"

"In the same way that everyone else goes about getting their refunds once they file for income taxes. They have funds directly deposited to their credit cards, their debit cards, or other forms of getting payment. Me personally, I also like to have physical checks mailed to designated addresses and post office boxes as well," he responded. With a clear tone of voice and one of the most remarkable masks he was able to fix his face into, Montell assured her with these eight words, "It'll be the easiest money you'll ever make."

At that point of him laying out the blueprint to exactly how the scheme was to be perfected and how the fruits of their labor was going to be reaped from the hustle, Verena looked him square in the eyes with such focus and intensity, that it scared him beyond his wildest imagination. For a moment, he thought he may had fucked up and incriminated himself right back into getting more time. But he hadn't. He was safe.

***

What did happen was, she related a few words to him that was straight as an arrow and nothing short of keeping it real in that instance.

"Nucca! If I have to say so my damn self your ass just *too* smart for your own good. And, you *too* damn slick in the way you go about convincing people to see things your way. You know how to utilize your abilities to force anyone to get involved in your acts. You're even better with the power of your word play, whether you know this or not. A person has to be very careful around a smooth talker like you, Montell. And don't you know that those goddamn white folks would have never thought for one minute that a nucca who's as big, black, muscular, bald-headed like you was, and street poisoned as you are, could have ever pulled off the type of things that you just laid out for me? You good, sir. Oh yeah, you-are-good!" She complimented ecstatically, as she unknowingly revealed more of her attraction to bold behaving men.

This slick-ass nigga Montell cracked one of the most sensational smiles he'd ever had the pleasure to put on display, and then uttered, "It was these same stereotypes that people hold against me and niggaz like me, that turned out to be the main weapons in helping me get ahead in the game from the very beginning." He managed to wisely use those detrimental remarks she reminded of to great advantage. She took no notice of the interchange.

Verena returned a smile of her own and gently placed her right hand atop his as he propped himself against her desk. She then snapped back to reality and reverted to the serious minded serious toned individual she had been at the beginning of their conversation. She gingerly eased her hand from his and then asked, "Well 'Mastermind,' you ready to do work and make more of that *easy money* you speak so fond of?"

Dude gazed deep into her bedroom eyes and replied very street and *gangsta*-like for her.

"Muthafuckin' right, I am! *Dafuq* you mean! Shit, just as sure as any hoe is that's on the block in twenty-degree weather, trying to sell pussy to pay for a meal and to pay her pimp from her day's work I am! The sooner you get me all the shit I need, the better. It's up from here, I assume?"

"Probably so. But, say no more. I'm on it."

The ball was in her court and she needed only to get him the information he asked for. And, from there, he would be able to take off like a G6 jet non-stop and make them some money like he was supposed to. It was definitely on and popping.

Chapter 15

Weeks Later...

The timing was in the middle of January, and tax season was almost in full swing. The better part about it was that Verena had begun to pass along the information to Montell of his fellow inmates he asked for. He was given fifty names at a time, so to be *"put to good use,"* in her words.

"I'll be sure to do just that. We know how to do this shit. We deep and well up to par—both electronically and with the old school format; mailing the claims in to the IRS. And, also, I need a cellphone upgrade too, so to better work with. I need something really good in order to help simplify my work."

"Something good to help simplify your work like what?" Verena retorted. This wasn't originally part of the deal. Montell got bold and slipped this one in on her.

"Something like a *Samsung Galaxy Note*. That's what. These types is my favorite. I prefer to do work on these. And I want the newest model Samsung Galaxy Note too. The shit that not long ago came out. And once the work is done, I'mma get rid of it by selling it to one of my niggaz for $1,000 or more, once I factory reset it."

"Understood. I gotcha," she verbally complied.

At any time Montell was not on detail and back in the dorm, he would use one of his personal phones. And this would only be every so often. He had almost always let his roommate or his closest homie, a guy named Snoop from

Albany use it, since Harold or Snoop, had responsibility of being his go-to-guys for stashing the phones while he was at work or enjoying a visit from his mom and sister. There wasn't any way Montell could have afforded to get caught with a cellphone, as this was a high violation and consequential piece of contraband. This would have surely blown his cover and exposed things he had going on below the radar.

His best bet was to remain as untouchable as possible. At least in the development stages of the business and personal bond between him and Verena. And once he thoroughly locked in, if it came down to it, he could easily have Verena overlook a situation and throw out the write-up. And at the same time Verena was sure to give Montell a few words of caution, now that the ball was rolling.

"Look, nucca, your black-ass need be careful down in that goddamn dormitory with anything you got going on, okay. And for damn sure, you better not slip and let one of the officers walk up on you and catch you with a phone or any other kind of contraband, Montell. But especially not a damn cellphone. I would hate to have to cut ties and let you loose," she stated.

The fact remained that, had Montell ever gotten jammed up in any way breaching security with possession of contraband item like a cellphone, he would have automatically lost his detail as an aide to Verena. Unless she made the write-up immediately go away, something she very well may do now, since they were in business together.

Also, by receiving a disciplinary report of any type dealing with rules violation, Montell more than likely would have had serious problems on his hands that was not in the control of the Verena. Certain Standard Operational Procedures had precedence over others. So, he was sure to keep all probabilities in mind as he pressed forward with Verena and standing on the business they were establishing.

***

In most of the prisons of the Georgia Department of Corrections, if an inmate is ever caught with a cellphone, he or she would be written up and sent to segregation, the hole, and also would stand the risk of being charged under state law, atop the punishment at the prison level. Not always though. And this was before cellphones became so widespread. The report then would be forwarded to the office of the Regional Director, Verena's boss, for any other recommendations.

Usually, more time gets added to the offender's sentence if found guilty of the infraction, or some form of restrictions applied. And there was no way Montell could have afforded any of this shit to take place.

He said to her, "Verena, we got serious business to handle, Ms. Lady. And there ain't no time for the bullshit to come in between. The both of us gotta be careful on how we interact and be perceived in and around your office. Haters are everywhere. You never know who. And we can't allow any staff members to become leery or suspicious of us. Simply put, as you would say, we gotta be careful," he let out.

"You're damn sure right about that. We can't get loose and become unmindful."

***

At the time when Montell mentioned the phone upgrade to Verena, he knew there wouldn't be any difficulty for her to make this happen when the time was at hand.

"Hey, I'mma need that phone upgrade at some point soon. You bullshitting with me about it. It's been almost two weeks now. And like I said—"

"You want the newest Samsung Galaxy Note. I got it. And you able to work better with one of these, not your old one. I kept this in mind. But nucca, tax season don't kick off until

January 31st anyhow. So chill," she cut in and said. "I should be able to make this happen. Just be patient and not be so eager to rush into things. You got this, I'm sure," She further added.

It's a well-known fact that in the Georgia penal system, any administrative official is allowed to bring their personal phones with them to work. That's especially true for the warden of an institution. Verena knew that Montell was aware of this fact, and there wasn't a need for him to have uttered a word about it anymore on how best for her to get it to him. She knew what to do. She responded to what he'd asked for. He only had to wait until she felt comfortable to give him the remainder of the shit he needed.

***

Throughout the time in the day Montell worked for more than a year from 7 A.M. to 4:30 P.M., he took careful notice that Verena indeed, was a calculated and meticulous woman like she said she was. She seemed to keep true to her nature in standing on the business she was about.

At the time they'd discussed the past actions of he and his crew, there must had been *something* that was said to really fascinate her and touched her soul in a way, he assumed. She turned out to have a lot of interest in things about him and began to show that she was down for the cause and the scheme he spoke on. She clearly wanted to fuck with him.

She reminded Montell, "Bad boys are *always* interesting to me. They are the ones who tend to come in first place. It's the bold and the handsome guys with the *Devil* in them— that's capital D—who we women want." Another confession.

Whether Montell paid her statement any attention or not, she'd blatantly gave him the keys to her heart and the gas necessary to light the flame of her soul. But as far as the business at hand was of a concern, Verena kept to her own script. She moved to the beat of her own drum. "I'm gonna *always* move how *I* move, and let you move how you move," she'd said. And whether directly or indirectly, Montell knew through her actions, that she was down for the cause. She was fucking with him. And also, she was eager to come through for them both. Each had to *deliver.*

***

Two Weeks Later...

After the game plan conversation, and her supplying him the printout of their list of "clients," they now had motion. Verena next brought to work, a brand new never activated unlocked cell phone Montell asked for, the brand he preferred. As expected, her keeping true to the airtight political stance she had and not incriminating herself, she placed the device into the top pullout drawer of her desk and left it halfway open so to show the front of it.

Montell was told by her to clean and re-organize her office, *"especially her desk,"* once she and the other staff members went out to lunch at the facility dinning hall for them. He'd began his work at the section where the file cabinet was in the corner and then worked his way over towards the desk, oblivious at first that there was a surprise waiting for him. He so happened to take a look down at the drawer and knew without doubt that the phone was there for him to grab hold of. The plastic was still attached to the screen and it was a clear indication that the device was new.

The only personal phone he'd ever known Verena to have, was the iPhone she always palmed and walked with. It never left her hand. "I don't prefer no other brand *but* Apple," she confessed. "I'm an addict of the Apple culture. Fuck everything else!" she proclaimed. "Oh, and I love the Dallas Cowboys. So, Apple and the Cowboys, it is for me," she remarked with a huge smile.

Montell had responded, "You see, *that's* the only area where we gonna bump heads at, because I fuck with

Samsung all the way. *Not* Apple. They're a competitor. And I love the New York Giants. **Fuck** the Dallas Cowboys! They're our division rivals," he emphatically came back with.

Verena laughed like hell at his words then said, "Mm-hmm. I hear you."

Verena and her staff were still out enjoying their meals in staff dining. This gave him time to grab the phone, put it in one of the trash bags he had that was half filled, and then, make it through the security gate before the noonday count was to begin, headed back to the dorm.

Once inside the dorm, he took the phone and passed it to the friend Snoop, until he was to return from work later. He had everything necessary in his reach and in place to handle the business and do the work that would make him rich again. This nigga was determined to make a million dollars. If it could be done once, it could be done twice. All thanks to his Verena, the silent business partner that she was moving forward.

Chapter 16

In Atlanta...

The brother of Roderick, a high—level heroin drug kingpin named Anthony Grady, better known on the streets of Philly as "A-One"—was in town. He wanted to surprise the baby boy with a pop-up visit, to at least see how he was doing, and to know what kind of progress the youngest son of their father was now making down south, fresh out of prison, and away from home still. Years prior, A-One, had put up the money to have him enrolled into college. The full tuition fee was paid in advance. Roderick did indeed graduate, but never did anything with the degree. He was versed in Business and Accounting Management.

A-One had a business proposal he wanted Roderick to hear. And maybe, he could convince him to start a business with the idea and his money. Or at least oversee expansions of his existing businesses.

Also, A-One was making it his business to keep out the way from the mean streets of Philly for the time being. At least until the dude who he wanted hit, had for sure been murdered and well out the way, and then, he'd return. A war was sparked between both camps. This was on A-One's, and Khalib Dumas' side of the streets. It wasn't safe for no one on either.

On arrival, A-One, a young girlfriend of his, and one of his vicious bodyguards, checked into one of the top hotels in downtown Atlanta the night before. They were at The Hyatt Regency on Peachtree. This is a five-star place to chill.

A-One, gave Roderick a call early in the A.M., around 7. He wanted to let him know he was there and more than likely would be for the next couple of weeks. A-One needed Roderick to put away any plans he may have had before the day. Because everything was now on him during his vacation, and Roderick didn't have to pay for shit. Just like old times. Big bro always handled the bills.

Roderick answered his phone at the notice of A-One's number, "Yeah, what up, bro. How you been? And what make you hit me up so early today?" he said. It was a Wednesday.

"I been good, lil bro. And what make me hit you up so early is because I'm in town now, nigga," he related with a hardy laugh and smile. "I'm in ATL. And gonna be for a few weeks."

"Oh, word!"

"Word. I took a vacation. It's me, one of my young *jawns,* and the homie BK. You remember him, right?"

"No doubt. The *boul* Brayden Knighton. Y'all two came up together."

"Yeah, you remember him. But anyway, I brought about one point five with me too. We gonna have some fun while I'm down here."

"So, where y'all at now?"

"We at the Hyatt. Downtown."

"Yeah, I know which one you talking 'bout."

"So, what time you pulling up, lil bro? We ready to get out and about, to see what all the A-Town has to offer us niggaz from Philly. Other than a gang of bad bitches, their country-ass accents, some good ass food, and it's *southern hospitality.*"

"Yo, I thought you say you had one of your young *jawns* with you on this trip?" asked the young brother.

"I do, nigga. But her ass still asleep up stairs in our suite. And me and BK, down here in the restaurant enjoying some breakfast. You know this my favorite meal of the day. Pancakes, turkey links, cheese eggs, and hash browns. And I gotta have my expresso too, ya know," A-One responded. "I'm working my laptop and phone too. Reviewing shit and replying to emails and other things."

"Gotcha. Always the attentive businessman. And when y'all get here?"

"Just after twelve last night. I booked the rooms ahead of time."

"So, you was already looking to surprise me, huh."

"That too. Other than me looking to be out the way, by the time my niggaz on the home front, handle the business we got going on with this nut-ass nigga we bumped heads with not long ago. He's gotta get it."

"Oh! That type of business, I see."

"Plausible deniability, lil bro. I was down here and don't know a fucking thing about it. Check with the Hyatt Regency Hotel in Atlanta, Mr. Detective. I used my bank card, and they got cameras everywhere."

"I know that's right. But check it out. I'mma go ahead and get up and shit. And I'll be there where y'all at in a couple hours, okay bro."

"That's a bet. We here. And keep in mind, I'mma be in your zone for the next couple of weeks. So anything you *had* planned, cancel that shit, bro. We gonna make new plans together."

"I ain't got no problem with that. Because, shit, I already know, everything is on you. And you already let me know, you brought along a bag to parley with. So, I'm all in."

A-One had to laugh at his brother's words to him. Roderick always loved when he liked to treat him to things. "I know that's right. And besides, I got a business proposition to put to you as well. I'm looking to expand with my vending machine company and my coin laundry business, 'A-One's Wash and Fold.' Also, my dry cleaners service. I figured that '*Hotlanta,*' could really use all of the above."

"Probably could. And this ain't a bad idea. To have establishments in Philly *and* here in ATL."

"That's exactly how I was thinking. But we can talk more once you get here. I'll see you then, lil bro."

"For sho.' Love you, bro."

"Love you too, Rod."

The call came to an end.

Roderick got up at that point and begin preparing for the day. He was really excited to know his big brother was in town, and they were going to spend time together. It's always a family affair for the Gradys.

***

Back With Montell...

For good reasons, Montell created a lot of fictitious social media accounts that were to be utilized on a certain basis. Say for instance, if he took a liking to a female on social media, and he wanted to pursue them, he would send a message through one of these profiles and await a reply. He believed that if he revealed to women he communicated with that he was indeed incarcerated, making the fact known in the beginning phases, he may would not have a chance at being able to connect with them and get to know them on a deeper level, had he not been truthful. He figured the best thing to do was to at least build up to a point with these potentials, then reveal his predicament later on. At least then, they'd be more involved and sympathetic at that point and continue on with all that had been started.

All of Montell's interactions with the many females he befriended online, was never done through any act of desperation on his part. It was more about him being lonely and in need of love and affection at certain points than anything. Reason being is because, before his imprisonment, there was three females he was involved with, but mainly one of the trio—Mandy Barfield, an attractive white girl— who was the one he found himself more in love with. Tamron was cool too. However, he adored Mandy.

About a year into his bid, Montell had to develop the emotional courage to tell her that he needed her to go on about life and live it without him in mind, because he'd pleaded guilty to the charges he faced, and had a sentence to serve. He didn't want or need her to slow down with her life for him, nor did he wish to ruin her life by having her answer to the demands that an inmate is subject to make.

"Mandy, look, okay. I got a prison sentence to do, alright. And I know you got a lot going good for yourself and in the career path you on. So, I'mma do us both a favor and let you go, okay. And once I finally get out, hopefully, you'll be in a position to where we can resume normal activities between us," he'd said to her.

As bad as he didn't really want to, he felt that he had to. This would at least give him a sense of peace and nothing to worry about by trying to keep up with a woman from a prison cell. Mandy cried and sobbed her ass off until she'd gotten it all out. The two ended the phone call with the respect between them both still there.

Montell was the convict who made terrible mistakes. This turned out to be a problem to his advancement in many ways. And Mandy truly had a bright and prosperous future ahead of her, and he felt it was best to let her go. The man simply had to, he felt in his heart. However, they still maintain a healthy contact and are good friends.

But Montell took to social media and checked out Verena's profiles again through one of his many accounts. He was bold enough to the point that he sent a request to be added on Facebook, then, he messaged her. To his surprise, she accepted and their online connection instantly began without her ever knowing that it was him. He knew it was best to keep everything that was going on at work, at work. This was how Verena wanted it anyway. Until at least, Montell delivered.

As time edged on, adding to the bond and dealings between the two, he sent her more messages every so often, to compliment her on a post she'd make or on the photos she would publicize, so to know exactly how far she would go. Montell's plays online helped him keep up with Verena.

Chapter 17

Not long after the day Verena printed out the information of the fellow inmates—522 to be exact—the true side of Montell began to reveal itself. And within the online conversations they'd begin, if she had only taken the time to pay attention to the facts and the way they were related, she would've noticed it was him, but she didn't. The attention she was given outweighed her recognizing the obvious. Not that he needed to go about doing things like this, it was that some old habits were hard to get rid of. This was one for Montell, keeping track of females online without them knowing it was him doing so.

Todd Debonair: *Hey gorgeous! How are you? There's something I wanna share with you if that's fine? To be honest, I really would like to be revealing, if that's a better way to put it.*

Verena: *I've been well. Yourself? Thanks for the compliment. What is it you might want to quote unquote "reveal?"*

Todd Debonair: *Well, we've been messaging off and on for a while now, and you have related valuable words of motivation and thoughts to me, no matter how brief they were.*

Verena: *Interesting way to put it, I must say.*

Todd Debonair: *I know and understand that you are a very busy woman. That's the reason I only breeze through every so often to say hello or to compliment you.*

Verena: *Yes. My free time is very scarce. Thanks for being considerate.*

Todd Debonair: *So tell me, what's it like being a female warden over an all-male facility? How do you balance the divide?*

Verena: *It's a bit challenging to say the least. However, I was thoroughly groomed for the task.*

Todd Debonair: *I admire how you keep things in such professional perspective. I find a strong attraction to that.*

Verena: *Oh really (smile emoji)?*

Todd Debonair: *Absolutely. Another thing. As a woman, NOT THE WARDEN, how do you maintain such high level of discipline, if you get my drift?*

Verena: *It's very much possible. I just keep in mind exactly what I'm going to do, as opposed to some of the things that a woman would like to do, you know (smile emoji).*

Todd Debonair: *Hmm. Nice come back. I never thought of it like that. You see how on point and deep your insight is?*

Verena: *Thanks.*

Todd Debonair: *Judging from your profile, I can't seem to figure out how some man hasn't wifed you yet, or why you have no kids?*

Verena: *That's a bit personal. But granted I admire your conversation enough. In due time, I'll be blessed with the above. For me, things simply has to be right well in advance. That's the way my parents did it and I intend to follow suit.*

Todd Debonair: *I wish you the best on that.*

Verena: *Appreciated.*

Todd Debonair: *Truth be told, I can't hold this back any longer. I wanted you to know the real me, the essential reality that is. I must reveal it no matter what the consequences may be.*

Verena: *???*

Todd Debonair: *I got the propensity to be a bold and audacious guy when I choose to be.*

Verena: *That type of energy may serve you well in the world we now live in this day and age.*

Todd Debonair: *I certainly hope so because here I go. I hold no fear of consequences because I can't keep doing it like this. Can you promise me that you will not get angry or chaotic at what I'm about to tell you?*

Verena: *It really depends.*

Todd Debonair: *Wait. Let me ask you this much first, before I reveal. Has there ever been a time any inmates ever attempted to contact you through Facebook or here on Messenger?*

Verena: *Inmates get busted all the time with cellphones. It's nothing new to me. Their incrimination on social media leads us directly to them. Some I spare, like first time violators, but most I don't, like repeat offenders. I have to condemn the repeaters. Why ask? And please don't tell me you're an inmate? I'm pretty sure that this 'Todd Debonair' is not an authentic account (lol)!*

Todd Debonair: *Let's say that if I was to confess and reveal the fact that indeed, I am an inmate, what type of damning impact would that have on our online conversation and exchange?*

Verena: *Ha! I'd probably laugh it off at first, then admire the fact afterwards, due to the boldness you showed (lol). But, if this be true, not only have you violated the laws of the state and the rules of the prison. But, you took things a step further by going after not just any ol' somebody that works at the prison. You made it your business to find a way to draw the Warden into a conversation which has carried on casually. I've got to respect that if nothing else. Notice I said 'respect' not 'accept.' This exchange would have only revealed certain things about myself that I've been completely oblivious of. That I'm indeed a hopeless romantic. It also shows how vulnerable I have become for the sweetness and kind words of an anonymous man (SMH). Only God knows best. By the way, exactly who are you? Are* *you willing to reveal that? May the sweet lord Jesus be my witness, I will not send the CERT team to get you. That will only cause more trouble and open the door to an investigation which is not necessary!*

Todd Debonair*: You promise not to have me sent to segregation?*

Verena*: I've just told you I wouldn't. What more do I need to say? Now who the heck are you?*

Todd Debonair: *You know what. On second thought, I'll keep it to myself on who I am. Just forget about it, okay.*

Verena*: You sapsucker you! But it's not a problem. It might be better that we keep things this way anyhow. I hope you agree.*

Todd Debonair*: I totally agree on that. And if it ain't broke, don't fix.*

Montell was almost at the point of revealing to Verena who it was she'd been communicating with. It's a good thing he caught himself. Verena would've not been too happy to know he'd walked a tightrope like that, with them being exposed on one side and her career being jeopardized on the other. It worked out for the best. He would continue to keep this little secret to himself. Verena would never know the true identity of this *Todd Debonair* fella'.

Chapter 18

Weeks Later...

Progress was being made. Montell did begin the preparations for the taxes immediately. He and his guys rather. Between the times, he would send Verena compliment or so here and there in her DM's. The *Todd Debonair* dude. She still hadn't realized it was him functioning as her secret admirer.

Montell was afraid in a way and had thoughts that maybe she would find out it's him and definitely block him from her profile, preventing any more contact. But she hadn't. He dared not send any requests for video calls though. But he figured that when the time did come, he'd be able to do all of this and more. He just needed to continue being patient.

His attention went back to the mission at hand—income tax work. Montell had gotten in touch with his lawyer, a Mr. Jeffrey E. Zeller III. His office was on Peachtree Street downtown Atlanta.

Montell said to him, "Mr. Zeller, can you set up an— 'attorney-client'—visit for us? I wanna go over a few things related to my convictions, and also, I need for you to explain the new tax laws that took effect since my incarceration, the parts about the filing process and all else that applies."

"I'm willing to do this for you, Montell. You're one of my better prepaid clients. Anytime, bud."

Mr. Zeller was asked to bring along a combination of various tax forms—1040 forms, 1040-EZ forms, 1099 forms, 4852 forms, and several blank W-2 forms. These were necessary to perfect the craft. Montell wanted to have a variety of formats of how they was filing, so to not create a pattern or cycle which would be easy for the IRS to recognize and blow their cover and indicate that indeed, a fraudulent scam was taking place. The lawyer continued.

"It's nice to hear from you again. Everything well with you?" the lawyer asked.

"Oh yeah. Just finishing up this time I got left. And I need your help on something."

"Is that right?"

"Yep. I'm lost in a lot of ways on the new tax code. I'mma need you to break it down clearly for me when you visit. And bring those forms for me. How soon will you be available?"

"I can't say right off. I gotta have a look at my schedule. It should be soon. Again, I can't say how soon though. How soon you need to see me?"

"Soon. Like in the next two to three weeks. I can give you extra, opposite the prepaid fee you already got. Basically, this money is something for your time. Because if need be, I'mma need the prepaid retainer fee to stay as is."

"Well, if you can do that, then I'm there next week. Where they got you at now anyway?"

"I'm done with my federal time. I'm actually only forty-five minutes away from you. If that much."

"Oh yeah. Where?"

"I'm in Buford."

"Oh man, that's an easy visit. I can call to the prison tomorrow to set everything up for next week. I was under the impression that you were still far off in another state serving your federal time."

"That's over with. But you call and set everything up. And between the time, I'll have the extra fee paid out to you soon."

"Sounds good, Montell. You take care up in there, okay."

"No doubt. See ya soon. And like I mentioned, I'mma need you to bring me a combination of those tax forms with you too. I gotta do mine. So don't forget."

The conversation came to an end. Montell was all set to consult with his lawyer again.

Additionally, the plan was to have the luxury of a number of physical checks mailed from The Department of Treasury to the addresses and post office boxes established for this purpose. Once they were to arrive, Montell's people would take them to the many check cashing joints, liquor stores, or elsewhere, to cash them using forged Power Of Attorney forms and get the money. A responsible person was designated for this duty. A rapport had long been established. Eric, as always, was Montell's go to man of their crew. He was perfect for the job. With him in the lead and Jamie playing second in command, they would be able to handle the business with ease.

***

One Week Later...

The workload duties with putting together the claims and filing them began on a Friday evening. Zeller did make it with those forms and gave his knowledge of the new tax laws. Montell started with the paper documents first. All of the tools were in his hands to work with, the phone upgrade, the list of names and information, the newly updated tax form instructions booklet he'd downloaded and had mailed to him, the debit cards information, and the post office box numbers, along with the addresses to the houses that checks would be mailed to. Of the 522 names and other personal information he had, Montell worked 200 of them himself and forwarded the remainder to Eric and Jamie and Roderick to process online. These dudes had it going on. They were rolling again like no other.

***

Montell and Roderick had a conversation after they'd completed the work. These two had talked leading up to the day, but not as heavily as Montell had with the other two guys on the team. Montell made the call.

"Yo!" Roderick answered at notice of Montell's number on the screen of his phone.

"Rod! What it do, my nigga! How you been? Me and you ain't really had a chance to chop it up like we should. Everything good?"

"Oh yeah. For the most part. Just can't wait 'til these names we put through come back with a payday for us all."

"Shit, you! *I'm* more ready than all three of y'all put together! Because my black-ass, need it the most."

"Just take a chill pill, nigga. Everything gonna work out in your favor. Watch. We got you. And I'm more than sure with all those names you hit us off with, we really gonna eat from them."

"I know we is too, my nigga. And I know y'all niggaz got me. Y'all been holding me down ever since y'all got out. I ain't got too much longer though."

"Nah, you don't. But shit, nigga, from what I now know, I hear you done caught some warden bitch up in there! Ol' sexy and smooth talkin' ass nigga, you!" Roderick said, letting out a laugh at the same time.

"You already know how I do, my nigga. Bag bad bitches and scam like hell as a hustle," Montell uttered with confidence.

"You always had a knack for the two. That's really your forte. That's your lane. And if you keep this shit up, nigga, I'mma nickname you 'Montell the Magnificent'," said Roderick. He laughed at his own wit. Montell did the same.

"That'll be cool too, nigga. At least I'll go down in the history books with a big name. Besides, that shit really fits my character. It's who I truly am... *'Magnificent'*."

Roderick damn near pee on himself laughing at Montell now. He then said, "Don't flatter yourself too much with that shit, nigga. I tilt my hat to you though. It was a compliment. Not a divine prophecy from God. And besides, my brother A-One was in town not long ago. You remember him, right?"

"Oh yeah. The long money having nigga with deep pockets. He paid for everything when we went to your city those times in the past. He's still *That Nigga?*"

"No doubt. Always have been. Always will be. And that's how he remember you. From those two times we all visited Philly back in the day, before we got knocked. You had a different female with you both times. And bro nicknamed you that shit back then, 'MontellThe Magnificent.' That would've been a dope ass pimp name for you if you was one, bro said. *Ha!* I'm just now telling you about it," said Roderick with another laugh. "He asked about you when he was here. Me, him, Jamie, Eric, and bro's homie, BK, all hung out when he was in town. He left, headed back to Philly a few days ago. But, we really had a good time while he was here. A really good time. I only wish you was here with us, my nigga."

"That's what's up. And I do too... wish I was out to have fun with y'all niggaz when your bro was in town. And come to think about it. I *did* have a different chick with me when we visited, didn't I."

"Yep. Tamron's feisty-ass the first time. And, that sexy-ass white girl Mandy, the second time. Bro said, you were a smooth and magnificent ass nigga when it came to the girls. 'Montell The Magnificent,'" he let out again.

They both laugh once more.

They talked for nearly forty-five minutes longer. Basically, game planning and going over ways on how to get money and go legit. Roderick told Montell all about the businesses A-One wanted him to establish there and all else. It was a productive conversation. All about the C.R.E.A.M. That's basically it. It was all about the money.

Chapter 19

Weeks Later...

All of the filings were properly processed with the majority of them passing through the system successfully. Montell was sure to keep checking on the status of the refunds by calling the automated service number. All was going smoothly. They were provided Friday dates that the expected payouts were to come through, with only a small number that were dated for Tuesdays. The difference between the days were, if you received a "Friday" date, that meant your money would be available the date mentioned. And if anyone got hit with a "Tuesday" date, expect no money, only a letter from the IRS explaining the problem and the delay.

Everything was looking sweet for Montell and company. There were 454 claims that had Friday dates. The man he'd trusted most to handle the business—the guy Eric—had it all under control. He was a *wiz-kid* at this particular hustle.

Before the refunds returned, brief phone conversations and text message exchanges through IG now existed between Montell and Verena. He took a chance and simply called her through one of his many fake accounts. Not the Todd Debonair one though. Verena admired his discreet movement and allowed him the contact. Although reluctant at first, he found a way with his words as always to get her to talk. It was on from there for real.

Then, the communications increased. "So, I now see you truly believe in me, more so than I gave you credit for. This let me know you trust me and respect me as a man. Because no doubt about it, Verena, you could've easily crossed my ass out and did me dirty. But you didn't," he said.

"Yes, I do. And no, I didn't," she replied to his statement. "I'm all in on the hustle, Montell." She'd gotten hungry for money. And didn't know how to curve this appetite no other way.

He said to her, "If there is one thing in the world I strongly believe is true, is that it ain't nothing that can't be negotiated. Period." This was a reality he knew firsthand. Everything was fair game. And appealing to the greed of a person, especially a woman—can prove to be an effective way to get things done, and done properly, and at the right time. The foundation to what he wanted to establish with Verena was somewhat shaky at first. But then, once the money indicator revealed that it was on the way, things began to change for the better.

***

Montell called through IG again on the night before the first installments of refunds was to hit. He wanted to report the progress. Verena answered. This was an audio call.

"Yes."

"Hey! What it do?" he greeted.

Verena smiled to herself at the thuggish nature Montell was letting on. "I'm well," she responded. Her replies were always very brief.

"Look, I ain't call to waste your time, a'ight. I called to let you know that shit done paid off," he informed.

It had gotten eerily quiet on the other end of the phone, much more than ever before when they talked. She had never said much. Very short responses. This time was no different.

"You there?" he questioned.

"I'm here," she replied.

"Check it out. Most of the names from the information made it through," he related.

"Hopefully that's a good thing then, right?"

"You better know it is! Shit is about to get really real from here. And don't be surprised if you see a different version of me going forward. A more hardcore street version of me. It's who I truly am. I had a role to play. Not no more. Money gonna change me, I openly confess. Maybe for the better. Maybe not. Who knows. I can't say. All I know is, I'm up again. I'm back in the game. But anyway, I got a phone number for you to call tomorrow, when you have the time. You already let me know you got a dentist appointment to get your teeth cleaned. So, I know I won't see you. But it's to my nigga, Eric. The both of you gotta set up a time and day to meet over the weekend. He'll have the money. A lot of it," Montell mentioned to her.

"Oh! Really?" she replied. Her energy more perked up now than ever.

"That's right. And whatever you do, don't let this money get to your head and change you. Forget about me changing. You just better not fuck me over, Verena. We up now! Together. You told me what the deal was with you, and I delivered. And I mean big time. You ready for the number?" he asked.

"Yes! Give it to me," she demanded, with more pep in her voice.

"Okay, it's four zero four, eight, seven, five, three, two, one, nine. That's my nigga Er—"

"I got all that. This is Eric's number. We have to meet," she retorted, as his words was cut short midway through his sentence. She reasserted her authority and high level of comprehension.

"I love the way you seem to finish my sentences and put things in perspective. Message me once you handle the business and connect with Eric," he said.

"Will do," she replied and then promptly ended the call.

All of the contacts between Verena and Montell took place through IG. He had not quite made it to the point of having her main number or her home address. However, he did have the upper hand over her in a major way. The majority of apps require the person who download them to allow access to their location on their devices. And with the Messenger app or IG one on an iPhone, if you don't turn off the locator, it will give others your exact whereabouts and pinpoint an address to anyone who you inbox or talk to.

Verena never turned off the locator on her iPhone, and Montell was able to search Google Earth for the address to her home in Buckhead, Atlanta. The thought never occurred to him to blackmail her or exploit the information that he had at his behest to do whatever with. He wouldn't do no shit like that no way. He wasn't that type of nigga by no means.

Montell liked Verena too much and had an intrinsic understanding of the esoteric nature of her spirit and the yearnings she had often struggled to reveal. Without revealing himself, Montell believed she knew that he understood her more so than given credit for. And based on this personal understanding, this allowed him time and opportunity to sift through her mental library, study her well, and then finally discover all she appeared to be about.

The both of them actually turned out to be more compatible in many ways than imagined, and also, had great chemistry. The road to prosperity and riches was theirs to stroll down in fashion and style. If anything, they were setting up one another to win and win big.

Chapter 20

On a business call, Montell said to Eric, "Look, E, you got responsibility as the leader of our small but effective crew, now. At least until I'm to make my return to the streets to regain the seat. And also, it's you Eric, more so than anyone, that I trust the most. Not saying I don't trust any of our other two homies. I just trust you the most. Your loyalty was never at question by any one of us on the team," he stated at the time.

"That's what's up, bro."

At the point of the money being available for withdrawal from the debit cards, those were deposited faster than the physical checks, Eric, Jamie, and Roderick, went around to multiple ATM locations throughout four different states in one day; Georgia, Alabama, Florida, and Tennessee, to clean off the debit cards. They had also bought a lot of high-priced items off Amazon with some of the cards for later resell. Yet, they bought riding lawn mowers and other big-ticket purchases from Lowes and Home Depot, to later resell as well. The goal was exclusively to clean off the money on the debit cards. There were a few physical checks that had arrived now, and those were bust down in the process.

Eric had the duty to see to it that each person involved got their fair pay one way or the other, as there were several people who allowed them to have checks and cards to arrive at their place of residence or to a post office box that they owned. Family members, friends, and businesspeople alike got their money of the tax pie. Everyone was able to eat and eat good they did, all at the government's expense.

The amount of money the claims produced individually was between $5,000 and $7,500. With the help of his guys on the outside, they all was going to eat good from the large operation. They hit for just over two million. Every penny they'd schemed for was nontaxable bread from the scam. Completely untraceable funds to them that were hustled up off the backs of the treasury and the IRS. Montell loved it.

Of course, the lion's share of the money had to be forked over to the Mastermind. This was Montell, so he felt. He and Verena were set to get one-point-two million, as the rest had to be paid out between Eric and everybody else. Montell marveled in thought, *Everything turned out to be not a bad return. Especially not for a dude that was locked away behind the walls of a prison, and having the privilege to direct the entire operation from the fucked-up predicament he found himself in. It felt so damn good to him to be winning again and back on top. It really did.*

Of the few people he'd become accustomed to talking with, Eric was that one somebody who he related a few snippets to of his personal business. He was certainly a solid dude who absolutely knew how to keep his mouth shut at all cost. Montell was able to say the same about Jamie as well, and also Roderick. But it's never a good thing to let people in on your business, no matter who it may be or what it's about. It doesn't matter how much you know them or how close you may assume the two of you to be, that's simply something you don't do. Period.

***

Anyway, Montell opened up to Eric and shared something with him about the things Verena and him had going on, amongst other things. He'd even texted Eric a few photos of her and encouraged him to check out the many others that she had available on Facebook and Instagram. Since the two of them eventually had to meet up at some point, in order for him to hand over the money that belonged to them, Montell knew the importance of having to establish a path of communication between the two, Verena and Eric.

He called Eric again to discuss the business.

"What up, Mo!" greeted Eric. "What it do, nigga!"

"Yo E. What's good, my 'waffle-colored' Negro brother?" he joked. This was about Eric's high yellow complexion of skin.

"Shit! Coolin'. What's good with you though, Montell? How you maintaining up in that piece, bro? I'm sure you can't wait to get free to burn some of this paper we've made, huh." Eric replied with a laugh and a slight chuckle.

"I know that's right, bro. A nigga can't wait to get free so I can spend some of that easy money we done hit for, playboy. Speaking of money, that's the main reason I called you, so we can set up a meeting between you and my girl, Verena so she can pick up," he said to Eric.

"That's what's up bro. And we had to put things off for a week so we could clean off the debit cards and shit. But it's all good now. You already know I'm here. By the way, how the fuck you get so lucky to catch a bitch like her, nigga?" he let out. "Montell you must don't realized that you hit the jackpot, my nigga?"

"That's nothing new for me, E. I bag bad bitches like her all the time, and you know this," dude replied in a rather cocky way.

"Yo nigga, again, you caught a warden bitch, my nigga! What other niggaz you know who able to do that type shit? Not many. If any who we know of. And, she's a high profile top notch woman of power, status, and position. You in the game for real now, nigga. Long gone are the days of ordinary street bitches we use to deal with. Now, I gotta make it my business to step my game up to match yours, or to outdo it.

You really did raise the bar on this one, homie," he said as he congratulated his friend on catching Verena.

"Yeah, that's all good and dandy, E. But guess what? At the end of the day, she's only another bitch with a piece of pussy between her legs that bleed once a month. She's another woman who got wants, needs, and desires, the same as other regular bitches do. No different. However, I do believe that Verena got low mileage on her though. But I won't really know until I finally do get the pussy myself. And besides, females, they're all the same, no matter the title, position, or status. Now check, I gave her your math. She should be calling sometime soon when she feel best to do so. But I told her about you putting things off for the time being to gather the money. I originally told her to get at you last week, but things got put off. Me and her still kinda fresh with the business, and I don't wanna spook her no type of way. The bitch might get the wrong impression and think it's a set up if I dictate too much. I gotta leave her with the free will to move and handle shit how she see fit, you feel me. I'm sure once you drop that bag of money on her for me though, *everything* will change for the better, and she'll know differently then. You feel where I'm coming from?"

"Hell yeah, nigga. I got you on that part. I'll be sure to let you know what the deal is when the time comes."

"That's real bro. That's real. But other than that, when you split the pot sixty-forty, you was sure to take care of everybody, right?" Montell definitely had to know what the business was.

"You got to know that, my nigga. I did everything accordingly," Eric replied with confidence.

"You treated yourself well?"

"For sho' nigga! How you gonna ask me some shit like that?" he responded. They both shared a laugh.

Montell continued, "Good. Now that the team is back in position to contend for the top spot in ATL in our line of work, we gotta be sure to keep up and not get fucked up like we did last time. And remember: '*Teamwork makes the dream work*,' nigga, because together, everyone achieves more. And each one of us play a part in getting things done," he stated to boost Eric's level of confidence. The kind that was in them both.

"Already, my brother. I love you Montell."

"I love you too, E."

"*Loyalty to the family until death takes us all.*"

Montell repeated Eric's statement then asked, "How's Nasha and your niece, Zakeya been, bro?"

"They good. Mom-dukes good too. And not long ago, I had to help Nasha out with some crazy shit that was going on. Some shit I gotta make you aware of when you get out. She got a crib up in Marietta now though. Had to get outta the city."

"Oh yeah."

"Yeah. But for the most part, she good now. I'll be sure to let 'em all know you said hello."

"That's what's up."

They ended the call.

***

Eric was born and raised in Atlanta, the same as Verena. Therefore, a meeting location for the both of them, couldn't have been a difficult task, since they knew the city well.

And to speak on city origins, again, Roderick mostly fly back and forth from Atlanta to his hometown and back again multiple times throughout the year. He did during their days in college.

Jamie was from Jacksonville, Florida. He was somebody who loved those sorry ass Jaguars NFL team. But everybody accepted one another and embraced with open arms. They'd spent plenty of time together, and especially so on the hustle and the grind. That sorry piece of shit Rico, wasn't worthy of being mentioned by them any longer, they felt. He wasn't shit to them anymore.

Chapter 21

Eventually, Verena did contact Eric, to set a time and place for the pick-up of the money. She dialed his number. The phone vibrated on his hip. He had no idea who it was calling him from such a strange number, so he ignored it at first. Montell previously mentioned to Verena that if Eric didn't answer when she called, she needed to send a text message to notify him who she was. She did so.

Verena: *Excuse me, does this number belong to Eric?*
Eric: *Maybe so. Depending who's asking?*
Verena: *It's Gordon.*
Eric: *Minor??? TF!... Oh! My bad. You mean Montell's friend, Gordon, right?*
Verena: *That's correct.*
Eric: *Oh okay... lol. I'm sorry about that. Didn't know who you were. Call me now please. I'll take it this time.*

Verena called once more. She instantly found something pleasant in Eric's voice as he answered. *Confidence. Boldness.* He was "silver-tongued" himself. The same as Montell. Only more cultivated and thuggish blended with his. He knew how to turn it up and how to turn it down. Montell didn't have this capability.

"Yeah! What's up! It's me, Eric here," he stated.

"Hey! How are you? I was told to contact you, to set up a meeting place," she stated in her formal tone of voice. She used proper articulation.

Verena was completely oblivious about how to relate with "regular" people, through conversation or otherwise. She did confess this before.

"Well damn shawdy! Pipe da fuck down a bit with all that technical shit will you! Sound too damn preppy. It's not like you about to have some type of high-profile meeting with the executive branch of the government, or with a *bougie* investment firm of muthafuckas' on Wall Street or something. You ain't gotta sound so 'astute' in speech. You too formal," he jokingly responded to her political correctness.

"Oh, I apologize, sir. I'm so accustomed to my career orientations, that I had forgotten to leave it where it was; at work," she said with a slight laugh to help her stiff ass loosen up a bit.

"Now, as I was about to say. You my nigga Montell's business partner, right?"

"Yes. I am."

"He speaks highly of you, I gotta say."

"Oh, he does?"

"Oh yeah. And why you flexing on me? You already know that shit. He says your professionalism is not matched by any other that he's met. And I gotta say myself, that he and I, have known each other for many years, and the guy has been involved with some of the best of the best in women on all levels this side of the Atlantic. I ain't never heard or seen Montell as head-over-heels about a female as he is about you. This nigga infatuated with you! By all means, he is. BY ALL MEANS!" he stated.

"Is this revelation a good thing or a bad one? And all we have is business together. Nothing more," Verena declared.

"What? So, it's just strictly business I see?"

"Yes, sir."

"Cool. But what the fuck. You fuck with us now. So, it's gonna always be a good thing. It's a *beneficial* and *meaningful* one too, as the three of us get more acquainted and conduct business together. But more on that at a later date and time,"

"When and where can we meet?"

"You know Atlanta pretty well?"

"Very much so."

"What about shopping centers you visit often?"

"Lenox Square Mall is my favorite."

"Cool! We can meet there this weekend. Saturday would be good."

"Sounds fine to me."

"We can enjoy a meal, maybe some ice cream or something too. And after that, I'll escort you to the parking lot to your car. I'll then pull next to yours and deliver the bag. It'll be two hundred thousand the first time and the same each meeting after," Eric advised.

"You'll have *two hundred thousand every time we meet?* My God! How much is the total?" she excitedly asked.

"Montell never mentioned to you the amount?"

"No! He only said it was a big score."

"Yeah, that's right. And if he never mentioned, it was because of *me* out here in these streets and the strings I pulled on my end to make it all happen. I'm the one who made this shit pop! Not him. But we'll have plenty of time to talk about all that and more. If you up for it?"

He must've detected some form of doubt Verena had in her about Montell for him to immediately put things out there the way he had.

"I caught that," she let out. "And I *might* be up for it," Verena uttered. *It depends on how you look and how well you're built,* she thought in mind. "But might I ask, exactly what are you implying, Eric?" Verena asked for clarity, as if she was seeking to resolve a grievance compliant filed by an inmate or a dispute between a pair of correctional guards that work for her at the prison.

"What *exactly* am I implying is that it was *me*—not him—who brought home the bacon and the bread, baby boo," he emphatically stated.

"Is that so?" she questioned. "And to be honest, I never fully believed Montell to begin with."

Bam! There it is, thought Eric. *I knew it.*

"I felt he might be only letting on half the truth. And I know he has the tendency to be a manipulator at times. He tries to talk too smoothly, and this comes off to me as attempting to be too clever, always looking to finesse somebody. But I see now the real truth finally comes out."

Or is it you Eric, who's the liar and the manipulator, the one who's looking to finesse? Verena thought again.

"Yeah. That's facts."

"Okay, that's another story by itself. One we could talk over another time. But I'll be available at two on Saturday afternoon. I'll text you to let you know when I'm there," Verena said.

"That's a bet. I'll be wearing a Golden State Warriors blue tee shirt and gold Under Armor sneakers by Steph Curry to match. You can't miss me. Me and that nigga both look just alike. You do know who that is, right?"

"Um, sir, I do live on planet earth... in America. Who doesn't know who Steph Curry is?" she sarcastically remarked in a way he'd clearly catch onto.

"No doubt. I'll see you then, shawdy," he lastly stated.

"Okay. Take care," Verena responded and their call ended, leaving her to think over a few things to herself.

I can't believe what I just heard! That boy just told me he's supposed to give me two hundred thousand each time we meet. HOT DAMN! That sap-sucker Montell done scammed the government yet again. Probably out of a million dollars or more this time too, like he had when he was out, and like it read in his profile. He's good. Oh yeah. Montell. He's really good, Verena thought over more.

Chapter 22

Eric and the future "scam-heiress" met up at the designated place as discussed. He was certainly intent on making it his business to treat Verena to a very nice time while at the mall. They met near the food court. He already knew what she looked like and approached from out of nowhere.

"Hey!" he spoke, startling her as she turned. A smile broke out across her face at how much he really did resemble the NBA star, Steph Curry.

"Hello! Eric, right?" *Damn! He looks like my ex-boyfriend Cannon from highschool too,* she thought. *How ironic.*

"No doubt," he responded.

"Wow! You and Steph do favor one another." Her smile was still holding.

"I agree. But let's cut to the chase. It's a reason why you're here. And also, I got *personal* reasons why I'm glad you're here," he stated so to implement a level of seriousness into the equation.

"Aw. You don't say."

"Oh yes, I *do* say. And so you'll know, in addition to the money I got for you for Montell, how about, I brought along a few thousand dollars of my own money that I wanna spend on you. But this will only be under one condition."

"That I not mention anything to Montell about it and keep things strictly between you and I, right?" she came back with.

Eric smile and then said, "I like how you finish up my words for me. It lets me know that we may be compatible in a way."

"Well, hey, I'm a big girl, if you must know. And I know how to keep my business to myself. I won't tell if you don't. Pinky promise on that," she let out with a smile and extended her well manicured right pinky finger. He did the same and they interlocked fingers, gazing deeply into the eyes of one another. Their smiles more affectionate now. Passionate even. Something in common was discovered.

"I see you got some flavor about yourself too, huh."

"I'm a southern Bella. Raised well. Thoroughly seasoned." "I like that. I really do."

Eric knew without a shadow of a doubt that Verena wouldn't refuse his offer. No woman would refuse a monetary advance of a man who through their intuition as a woman, told them that the man was in hot pursuit after them. And besides, Eric had a striking level of handsomeness about himself that appealed to her. His swagger in dress code and pleasant features sent shock waves of sensation shooting up her spine. Verena was instantly turned on by dude. At first sight.

"So where do we start with this offering you say you got you wanna spend on me?"

"Wherever you would like for us to start, sweetheart. Wherever you like."

The two then began to take a stroll through the mall in the direction of the department store Verena loved most in this particular shopping center: Neiman Marcus.

As they roamed the interior of the store, the conversation really took off between them. "So, tell me more about how it was that *you* per se, and not *So and So...* made the whole thing happen?" Verena asked, intentionally eliminating the use of Montell's name from the equation so as to not feel guilty in no type of way or inadvertently back biting him or slandering him.

Eric caught the hint. It's not character assassination if no name is mentioned.

"My pleasure. So here is what happened. It was *So and So* who reached out to me and said that he got lucky and caught a *warden* chick who he worked for at the prison."

"I. Know. He. Didn't! And how did he just jump to such a conclusion like that?"

"I don't know. I can't tell you. But he said that he'd been working for you for just over a year. Dude also said that you was a gullible wannabe high class hopeless romantic, with no dude in your life, and, that you was easy to finesse."

"He said all that about me?"

"*Humph!*" he scoffed. "Did he?" I was assuming he really did his homework on you. Everything about you on your social media profiles, he learned. And then, before long, he told me all about how y'all two use to talk in your office all the time and how interested you was in him."

"I wasn't *that* interested. That nucca really feeling himself, ain't he! But go ahead. Continue please."

"He said you knew he was a really smart dude and all, and begin asking a lot of questions about how *he* per se, finessed the government out of all the money he made in the smooth was that *he* did. And how could *he* help you get rich. In his words, you asked, '*what all did he need to make you a rich woman... mastermind?*' And this was the point when y'all really got going. You gave him the personal information of five hundred and twenty-two other inmates. After this, the same week actually, you brought him a new phone. A Samsung Galaxy Note. The bottom line is this: the nigga told me everything."

Verena simply looked on at Eric in a horrified way. "He wasn't supposed to do that. But anyway. Keep going."

"Well, he did. But now that I know, here is what I want you to do. Because we already too far into it, to have the nigga get grimy and turn and fuck everything up," he said. "If it ever gets to the point where he's pressuring you to fuck him... you need to do it. And that's simply on the strength of us now not knowing what the nigga could potentially be capable of. So, at all cost, don't deny him. You can *stall* him to the best of your abilities. But, don't deny him, if push ever came to shove. You got me on that. Least this'll keep your ass out of handcuffs and away from a courtroom, if he ever get in his feelings and wanted to harm you."

"Damn! I gotcha though. I'll be mindful of this moving forward."

"Good."

The thought of Montell telling someone else all of their business wasn't a good thing for Verena. A feeling overcame her like if she didn't cooperate, Montell could use everything he had to blackmail her. But at the same time, Verena also knew that at no time, had she personally handed Montell anything. No list of names. No cellphone. Nothing. She'd left whatever for him situated on her desk, the phone and atop her desk, the list of names and information. If anything, Montell *stole* this from her. She had no knowledge of it.

***

Their conversation continued. "Look," Verena let out, never mind anything that So and So has said, okay. He's making stuff up. He's trying to make himself seem more important in your view and more connected to me than anyone could become. But like I said, pay that no never mind. And I'm here with *you* now. Where he at? He's not able to spend time with me or any other woman right now for that matter. *You* are. He's not the one buying me expensive gifts and having a casual conversation with me and getting to personally know me. That's *you*. So, let's keep our energy and focus on what *we* got going on. You and I exclusively," she said, her mind now on that $200,000 bag Eric had already revealed he had for her.

If Verena was as smart as she presented herself to be, she could've played them both to get more money out of each and neither of the two would know a thing. This may was her plan all along from that point moving forward. She was hellbent on finessing the more finesse one, whether Montell or Eric. She'd soon find out.

"We can do that. Let's forget any and everything that dude has said and continue to focus on who we are, and what *we* might be able to establish. And you right. It's not *him* out here with you. It's *me*. And I feel privileged," Eric let out, posting an immaculate smile. He caused Verena to glow in admiration. She was feeling him more and more as the time they shared progressed.

Eric treated her to expensive gifts and made a damn good first impression of himself beyond her wildest imagination. Over their meals and pleasant flavors of ice cream, he was truly able to serenade Verena like no other, through the power of his intimate word play and passionate attention he gave her, Eric painted a magnificent picture of himself with his eloquent yet thuggish speech, and was able to magically removed Montell altogether from the equation, situating himself as the man of the hour and at the forefront like Verena had already done. This was a stroke of genius on his part by all means in the world of seduction.

***

Eric wanted to know more about her personal life and how she was brought up. He began down this path by asking, "So tell me, who is the most important man you ever had in her life? Most females will say it is their father. Who do you say?"

She revealed this, "Yes. For me, it's my father too."

"I figured that. But since we on the subject, what about your parents? Tell me about your dad first. Since I'm sure he has to be an important figure of a man in your life, as you said."

"I ain't got a problem with relating my personal life to you, Eric. In fact, I take pleasure in doing this. But, my father, his name was Robert Francis Gordon. He careered as an engineer, working at the Coca Cola Company here in Atlanta for many years. Tragically, my father was killed in a terrible car accident that was caused by the driver of an 18-wheeler. The trucker had dosed off to sleep and fatally rear-ended my daddy as he attempted to exit the interstate. Daddy's car was forced over the guard railing and into a steel light post, exploding into a blazing fire. He was on his way home from a Masonic Fraternal Hall meeting that dreadful night," she said. A tear streamed down her cheek from emotion she'd felt at the thought of losing her father.

Eric tenderly wiped away the tear drop and said, "I'm sorry to hear this. My condolences to you and yours."

"I appreciate that, Eric. I really do."

"No problem. And your mother?"

"My mother's name is Deandra, but everyone calls her simply 'Deanne,' or 'Mrs. Deanne.' She formerly worked as Deputy Clerk of Court for the Fulton County Superior Court, before retirement. My momma never married again after the death of my father. And according to her, no other man would ever measure up to the stature of a man her Robert was. My father was the only man she'd ever known, as the two had been together since their days of middle school. That's a long ass time together."

"It damn sho' was, *fuq* you mean, ha ha ha," Eric worded, and they shared a laugh to sort of smooth out the emotions associated with talking about her father's passing.

"But the settlement from the lawsuit with the poultry company Tyson's the driver of the big rig worked for, along with the pension and life insurance policy of my father, blessed me and my mother well. The resources paid off our home daddy situated us in. It also paved the way for the floral and garden shop my mother had always dreamed of having. I was only twelve at the time of my father's death. I really miss him," she stated.

***

Eric gained the upper hand over his business partner and so-called "*friend*," in the terms of properly coaching Verena on how to invest the money and appropriate the cash in multiple ways. As opposed to simply having her to "go and pick up large amounts of cash" without a game plan on how to situate the money and not violating the law. Montell somewhat had the *"Floyd Mayweather Jr syndrome,"* pay cash for everything, and spending his riches for any and all. To hell with properly investing in realistic assets. But after all, in America, Cash Is King!

The Whiz Kid Eric turned what was only intended to be a twenty-minute meeting into a four-hour rendezvous. He was helpful as an adviser to Verena, as she became able to build a rapport with him in a far more progressive way than with Montell. At least this how it appeared. This was due to the unfortunate circumstances and dire situation that the imprisoned friend found himself in.

But, the fact remained, Verena was supposedly *Montell's woman*, in his mind, and also, *his* potential wife to be. And it was him that had formulated the scheme that made them rich. It was his idea. Not Eric's.

The unquestioned trust that had been placed in Eric had begun to fall apart. A chink was created in his shield of loyalty. Eric wouldn't have never thought of doing such a thing in the times of the past. But people change. For better or for worse.

A woman and a few bucks are always the reason behind a gap being put between two male friends. And in most cases, there is never a way to reconcile any of the differences that may pop up.

Montell and Eric had known each other and dealt with one another for quite some time before the seeds of separation was planted. But if Verena knew any better, she could've continued to fulfill the role of being the good friend to Montell, as she put herself in position to be. That's only if she knew the stage well and worked hard at the craft. Only time would tell as a potential battle loomed.

"I wanna thank you, Eric," she said to him as she was getting in the car. "I had a wonderful time with you today. A *really* wonderful time. And I must say, you favor a boyfriend I had back in high school. His name was Cannon." She spoke sincerely to him, as he opened the car door for her and wished her well. The bag of money was put in the trunk of Verena's car already.

"Oh, I do? Maybe that's a good thing."

"It is. It most definitely is." Her smile was wide and enticing.

"And I had a really good time today with you myself, Verena. And I really appreciate you for being open with me and letting me know about your family. This is personal to me as it is for you. No need to worry. I won't utter a word to no one. Okay. My word to God on that. And a *'Pinky Promise'* on that too," he stated, extending his hand himself this time first and easing in closer for a possible kiss. They simultaneously locked fingers and lips to seal the deal. It was on and popping from there between the two.

Chapter 23

The Very Next Day...

The impression Eric made and the meeting itself Verena had with him was heavy on her mind. She felt so special and privileged, to not only be catered to and having a man spend his money on her for a change. But the $200,000 bag that Eric dropped on her, along with the sentimental gestures of a gentleman he presented, was enough to make her say *"Fuck it! I'mma take a chance now and throw the dice. On both... love and lust!* And this, she was willing to do. Immediately!

In addition, thoughts of Eric, his voice, his amazing physique, the brilliant intellect of his in culmination with his Atlanta street swagger, his game tight level of articulation, and, his hustle and grind mindset and ambition, made for a restless and fantasizing night for Verena.

The tender touch of his lips and the firm grip of his hands on her ass cheeks, had her enthralled and craving more. *I'll definitely give this nucca some!* she thought. *And you know what! I AM, gonna give him some! First thing in the A.M. I will! If he answers his phone for me and is willing to come over and fuck me!* She declared the night before.

Verena hadn't bust a nut since good God knows when, and, she was so backed up, to the point of being willing to give her a hole of honey, to a random nigga she'd only met once and knew nothing about. Talking about winging it and living life spontaneously, Verena, contended in position to be the epitome of this, and felt good about doing so. But at the same time, there are certain type of dudes in the world that have this type of sex appeal and power to make women do these kind of things without doing nothing at all themselves, other than being themselves. Eric proved to be this type of immaculate nigga, in the eyes and in the mind of Verena.

The time was eight on Sunday morning. Verena and her mother was up like always to prepare for church. This was an every week thing, but especially so on this day, being the first Sunday of the month. Hours earlier, Verena already made the decision that she wouldn't be going. There was another Sunday service that was about to be in session. One she would be host of, and her guest, would be the one to talk all the good talk and preach the gospel between her legs, with his magic stick and his sanctified movement in body language.

She texted Eric.

Verena: *Good morning to you, sir! Hope you slept well (smile)*

Not even a minute later he replied.

Eric: *Good morning to you as well. And yes, I did rest well. Had you on my mind. But. What's on your mind though? Talk to me.*

Verena: *I'll be honest with you. Everything about you and our "date" yesterday, has been on my mind. You swept me off my feet, Eric. And I ain't never had a man do that before. I like it! I love it! And I want more of it! (Smile)*

Eric: *You don't say. And that's what that was yesterday, a "date," you say? (Smile)*

Verena: *Oh, hell yeah! (Lol) That's exactly what it was. Anyway, I didn't disturb your rest, did I?*

Eric: *Nah. You good. I get up every morning at 3:30 anyway. But, what's up though?*

He urged her to tell him what it was she wanted. To spit out what it was she had on her mind to say.

Verena: *You available for a call?*

Eric: *Sure. Hit me up now.*

She immediately made the connection.

He answered, "Hey!"

"Hello! And it's a pleasure to hear your voice again," she responded.

"It's a pleasure to hear yours as well."

"I'm gonna be honest, Eric. You rocked my world. You really *fuck* my head up yesterday. And just to be real with you, I wanna see you again," she stated. "Like ASAP!"

"When? And I ain't talking about us meeting up again for me to drop off more money to you for another nigga! I'm talking about us meeting up again, for me and you to lock in more. Because I loved how tender and succulent those luscious lips of yours felt. And now, I wanna know how that nice ass of yours feel again in the palm of my hands, while I'm kissing you, and making you feel good all at the same time," Eric says, making his desires explicitly known.

Verena reply to him, "You really do make me feel special with the way you talk to me and treat me. With the attention you gave to me as well. And because of this, I want you to come over to my place for a little while. And I mean like, come over to my place *right now!* I live in Buckhead. I'm texting the address as we speak," she stated.

"I'm on my way out the door right now. I'll call you once I'm out front your house."

"Okay. I'm waiting on you. Lord knows I can't wait to see you again."

"I feel the same way about you," he came back with.

The call ended.

Eric knew this had to be a "booty call." And he'd never had a booty call this early in the A.M. like this, let alone, early on a *Sunday* morning. This was a first, and he was all for it.

Verena went back to help her mother finish getting ready for church. They both are members of the house of worship that Tiffany's husband's father own. Tiffany's mother and Mrs. Deanne, are good friends.

"'Rena, why you not getting ready, baby?" Momma Dee asked. "You not going or something?"

"No, momma. Not *this* morning. But I'mma be sure to give you enough money to put in the collection plate. This should make Bishop Long overlook and excuse my absence. At least for *this* day," Verena said then handed over to her mother a $2,500 roll of $100 bills. "Here, this should do the trick, I believe."

Mrs. Deanne graciously accepted. She then said to Verena, "Well, whatever your reasons are for not going today, I sure hope they involve a man somewhere in the mix. Because I'm so ready to see you get married, and I have me some grand babies to run behind and clean up after, that I don't know what to do," the mother remarked.

Verena smiled in excitement as she and her mother held strong eye contact. "You just may get your wish. You just may," she came back with, now positioning herself to zip up her mother's dress, but was only half able to do so, since she had her phone in one hand awaiting on Eric to call once he'd gotten there.

Shortly thereafter, a text message alert came through. It was dude... *That Nigga* who Verena now had in her life. Her blood raced through her veins. An ecstatic feeling overtook her body. And in addition, her pussy tingled and throbbed. Her moment of truth to show and prove was at hand.

Eric: *I'm here. I see your car so, I know I'm at the right house. (Smile)*

Verena: *Okay. On my way to the door now. (Smile)*

She picked up the pace in attending to her mother and said to her, "I got a friend I want you to meet, momma, before you go off to church." She turned to make steps towards the front door at that point.

"Oh! You do?" Verena looked back over her shoulder and smiled.

She opened the door so that Eric could lay eyes upon her. He got out, standing tall at six foot three, dressed in a fitted sweat suit of the college he attended, and made steps towards Verena's direction in a fresh pair of Nike Air Jordan's 1 Retro, white, gray, and blue in color.

The two embraced, gazed deeply into the eyes of one another, and then kissed slowly and with sense of purpose.

"I'm so glad you can make it," Verena said first.

"I'm so glad I could, too," he worded with a bright smile.

"Come on. Let's go inside. I got someone I want you to meet."

"Cool."

They held hands as Verena escorted the light skinned gentleman into her home. She was delighted to do so.

Mrs. Deanne appeared from the back.

"Momma. Say hello to Eric. And Eric, say hello to momma, please."

"Hello, son!" the mother uttered.

"Hello, ma'am. Nice to meet you," he said, extending his hand to shake hers.

"Nice to meet you, too."

"And momma, more than likely, you can look forward to seeing him around here more often, okay."

Eric took a look at Verena behind her comment. His smile was wider now. "Is that right," he responded.

"Mm-hmm," she confirmed, smiling more herself.

"That'll be wonderful. It's about time." The mother's humor was well received. It caused them both, Verena and Eric, to let out a laugh.

"Okay, Eric's gonna go to my room until I finish helping you get ready, momma."

"Okay. And I look forward to seeing you, Eric. You're welcomed here anytime, son," said the old lady. Her impression was that Verena and dude had been involved for quite some time now. She had no awareness that they'd met not even twenty-four hours earlier.

Verena then led him to her personal space, had him get comfortable on her bed, and returned to her mother.

Not long after, the house phone rang. It was Tiffany calling to notify them she was out front to pick up Mrs. Deanne. Verena answered. She'd already mentioned to her the morning of that she wouldn't be going to church today, let her know exactly why, and asked of Tiffany to swing by to get her mother for her, so she could be present.

"Momma, Tiffany is out front waiting on you. Here's your purse. And don't forget to let Bishop Long know, that I'm making this generous donation on the both of our behalf, okay."

"Will do, baby. And I'll see y'all two when I get back, okay."

"Okay, momma," Verena let out, kissing her mother on the cheekbone and handing her, her purse while she exited the door. She peeped her head out to wave hi to Tiffany, Tiffany's mother, and Tiffany's daughter Chastity.

Once closing the door, she eagerly turned and fast stepped back to her bedroom where Eric was parlaying at. He had the TV on ESPN Sports Center. He got to his feet when she entered.

"So, I'm back," she said with a smile and gazing at dude. She then made her way over to the nightstand where she'd sat her phone and programmed it to the special playlist she often listened to. *No Ordinary Love* by Sade began to set the mood. "I've had this moment on my mind all fucking night. If only you knew."

"Just like this, hmm," he said, holding a smile that had Verena spell-bound. "And I can imagine how much you had this moment on your mind. It's crazy but, so did I. My dick got hard as a muthufucka' when I first looked at you."

"I saw that," she proudly said with a big smile. "You holding too. That's one of the main reasons why I couldn't wait to welcome you here."

"That makes it all the better, now doesn't it? Already having an attraction and being aroused.."

"It damn sho' does."

"And so you'll know, I don't have a care in the world this day. There's nothing holding me back. Because, honestly Eric, I wanna get loose! I wanna be naughty! Maybe a little reckless for a change with my spontaneous nature. And, I wanna go back to being the thoughtless *thot* all over again, the one who I once was twenty plus years ago in high school. At least for today. And on top of that, I've been a hopeless romantic with a dirty, perverted, curious mind. So, truth be, I hope you understand."

"Oh trust me, I that shit. And there's nothing wrong with getting with the program every now and then like you really wanna do. Sometimes, we gotta get loose and live a little, you know. That's simply in our nature."

"Well, good. I'm glad you see things the way I do. And here." She presented Eric with three condoms. "Hopefully you're built to go through all of these in the next six hours," she stated, smiling wildly.

They then hug tightly and begin to tongue-kiss passionately. The foreplay got going, then the undressing.

Verena went down on him and took dude into her mouth. It was on and popping from there. The taste of Eric's dick in combination with the size, brought out the *super* freak in Verena.

Chapter 24

Meanwhile...

The scam master Montell was all smiles and happy as he could be once Verena let him know that the first drop of the money had been picked up. The type of happiness this nigga felt was similar to something that's felt on New Year's Day or for 4th of July celebration. The likes that would include fireworks, gunshots, crazy wild sex, and all else. There was nothing that brought a scam nigga like Montell joy and an intense level of energy as do a move that had paid off big. They'd "hit a lick" and was determined to blow a check!

Before Montell was able to use the information of his many fellow inmates, he had never benefited from any type of scheme or other operation so large as that at any one time. The detail he had in working for Verena as an aide, turned out to be a Godsend and a blessing in disguise. The scam was a big one, and also, a major crime by the book. Montell did it all from a prison cell. He strongly believed that what he'd done belonged in the same conversation as the move made by the guy in the *Shaw Shank Redemption* movie. That no one should ever underestimate the power and the ability of a prisoner's mind. Period!

The door was opened again for him to make money scamming. This was how he knew best. This was also an opportunity for them to get more serious paper. All they needed to do was use money from the first scam to pay their way with the next. Montell and Verena as set to do well together. If only they didn't get greedy.

***

Montell took immediate notice in the different ways of how Verena began to treat him once she had the money with her. She knew without doubt from that point forward, that the man was official. But so was Eric now. And, that he was for real. So was Eric too now in her world. She catered to Montell in a special way and cared for him as if he was royalty or something to the effect. She also did this with Eric when off from work. But maybe her treatment towards Montell was her keeping true to the words Eric mentioned to her about not making Montell feel less than.

Of course, Montell knew how to continue in playing his part and adapt to the role in the eyes of others. He also managed to maintain in mind that she had a job to do. It had to be carried out right. And at the same time, he had a sentence to finish up. However, any time the two had the opportunity to have a moment in private, the *real Verena* would show up and the *Warden* would temporarily disappear. This act got better with time.

Montell was more than sure at the time it was made known to her that the process worked and the information was good, along with the money being available for pick up, he'd really convinced her in a major way to believe in him more.

During the conversation they had when she was told to meet Eric, Verena's controlling ass, probably creamed all along the inside of those silk laced panties she wore. Montell was sure she had had some type of euphoric release, based on how ecstatic she seemed.

Money is the thing to make this bitch cum, I see! he thought. It wasn't no doubt in Montell's mind about this.

If there was one thing Montell could honestly say and be proud about throughout the whole situation, he knew for a fact he'd proved himself. He'd proved himself to be a serious man and capable of producing money he had always bragged about being worth. And it was at this particular point when the foundation to something intimate began to take shape. This part of what they had was put into motion.

There is nothing in the world that situates a man in a better position with a woman than does making her stable and financially free. There isn't one woman in the world who prides herself on being strictly about their business, that wants anything to do with a broke man. Not one is known. The belief for Montell was rooted in the fact that Verena had really given herself over to him. She had become his lady without needing to say it. Or so he thought. This was Eric's instructions playing out.

"So did I prove myself to you with everything I said before the money hit, Verena?" He asked.

"You did. We good, Montell. Just continue to be cool and allow things to flow smoothly, okay. It's no need to prove yourself no more than you already have. You got my attention," she said.

"You can stall him to the best of your abilities. But, don't deny him, if push ever came to shove." She thought over Eric's words.

"Thanks! That's all I needed to know. Now all we gotta do now is be patient until next tax season and do this shit all over again."

"So that's what the plan is?"

"Oh yeah! Ain't nothing like the second time around, sweetie. You'll see."

It was a fact that he was able to trust Verena now with their money, as he believed all of it was in good hands. Other than the money, she also had the duty to protect him from any form of prosecution that could potentially threaten his approaching freedom behind the scenes. Reason being, even though Verena didn't have anything hands on to do with the scam, there was still much that lingered. It mandated a cover up, to be kept out of the way from any potential investigation that could be launched.

Not only was Verena the warden of a prison, but could it be imagined how huge the storyline would be if a scandal of this type was to ever leak out and become exposed? Those fucking greedy ass pigs that are her superiors and other higher ups, would surely castrate Montell's black-ass behind it, and then, have him shipped off to the "super Max" prison in Florence, Colorado. Atop that, they would more than likely behead Verena's ass for such a high-level act of treason by joining forces with an inmate, of all people, and had not allow their greedy asses the chance to get a slice of the illegal pie the scam produced.

There was many higher powers that be who would certainly want in on a payoff that was made possible through a low-risk scheme by a person who's considered a "crook-by-the-book." Rather that be a kickback percentage, or an illegal lump sum handout. Without question, most would want in on it. After all, it was the "big wigs" that appointed Verena to the position. Also, it was them that wanted to utilize her to keep people like Montell in check.

In a sense, the superiors had power and control over her, as they ordered Verena around on all she was to do. But, at the point of her being in contact with Montell and him providing her with the type of money her job would take four to five years or more to provide her with, Verena became more than convinced that her financial freedom and future was brighter with Montell and his schemes, Eric's too than it was with them, the Department of Corrections.

***

In The Meantime...
The newfound level of respect established by Verena for Montell and also Eric on the side was earned in a major way.

Money was the motivator, and money was the glue that bonded them together. The main goal Montell had in mind, after the money, was to have her become interested in other things. To maybe become emotionally attached to him in some type of way. He wanted her to splurge.

"Verena, look. You got my permission to take some of the cash from my portion of it, and do what you feel necessary, to expand the floral and garden shop you and your mother own, okay. And in addition, I'mma need you to establish a small-scale real estate LLC that the both of us could benefit from at some point in our future. How that sound?"

"Sounds like a plan to me. I'mma do just what you gave me leeway to do."

This was something they'd discussed while she was at work, holding the real portion of what they really wanted to say for when she got off.

The two held a deeper conversation this night. It was all in the day's work. "Verena, here is what I want you to do, okay. I know I told you, you have my permission to do what's necessary business-wise. But, I also want you to really treat yourself to something nice with some of the money you holding onto, okay. And as a matter of fact, I want you to go out and buy a new car. Your choice. There. You got my permission," Montell said.

"Why thank you!" she responded with a loving smile. "It'll be my pleasure to. I was wanting a new ride anyway. Now, I got the leeway to go and get me one."

"Yeah. You do that. And while you're at it, I'm gonna need you to put a little something more on a couple of start up businesses for us. I wanna see us grow to become entrepreneurs in the world. This ain't too much on your plate, is it?"

"Not hardly. I can make this happen."

The conversation continued on for the better part of an hour. It was mostly pleasantries expressed towards her by him, to keep her interested in all he wanted. As if all that money wasn't enough. This was on a Saturday afternoon, and Verena was home chilling and relaxing, contemplating over it all.

***

She'd earlier called Tiffany to come over and they have drinks. She'd showed up not long after Verena's phone call with Montell ended. The two ladies were seated and situated to have a deep talk. The smooth lyrics of *Bryson Tiller* played in the background. Verena loved his music. Tiffany didn't hesitate not one bit in jumping straight into the subject that was on her mind.

"So, bitch, who the *new* nigga you fucking with in now day and age? Catch me up on the happenings. What's tea? It's been a minute," she said, referring to Verena's relationship status. "And so, you'd know, momma Dee, said something to me already. So, spill the tea, bitch, spill it," she said, now smiling with heavy anticipation.

Verena looked on at her and smiled gleefully herself. The two kept no secrets from each other. No matter how severe or full of consequences they were.

"Honestly, Tiffany, I ain't been nothing but a hopeless romantic of late. One with a dirty, perverted, and curious mind. But... you sure you wanna know about this one?" she let out ruefully.

"Ah, duh! I asked, didn't I, bitch! Now give me the tea, Verena, because I'm thirsty as hell for it, you hear me! Your ass got all this new shit laid around. A brand-new Cadillac and shit on your mind to buy. New items in your home. What nigga in this world you done put that pussy of yours on, girl?"

"Well, *technically*, I ain't gave the goodies to the one who I *thought* made all this money stuff happen for me. At least not yet. But I *did* give it to the other one who claims to be the official mastermind behind the work that brought home the bacon." Like always, she chose to be careful with her words.

Amused yet confused, Tiffany shook her head rapidly and let out, "Huh! What the hell does all that mean, 'Rena? And stop speaking gibberish and talk straight to me, boo-boo! Come on now, this is *Tiffany* you talking to."

Verena smiled ecstatically at Tiffany's witty comeback. Teeth showing and the whole nine. She then went on to relate only so much about all that was going on between her, Montell, and the rendezvous she had with Eric on two separate occasions. The second meeting was *really* the one.

In conclusion of their conversation, Verena said to her, "Here girl, this should help you out with everything, you know. And don't *ever* say I ain't never gave you anything." Verena smiled at the point when she blessed Tiffany with $50,000 in cash. She then vowed to that it wouldn't be too much longer before she would start up a small business, and have Tiffany serve as the C.O.O. Tiffany was excited about all this. But honestly, Verena was greasing her palms for two good reasons: one, to keep her mouth closed about what she now knew; and two, she really wanted to have Tiffany win in life right alongside her. She was the sister she never had.

***

About the business she had told Montell she'd do, Verena said to him, "I'mma make it my business and venture out and make the investments into those franchises you want me to. I'mma do them through my investment app I got, *Robinhood*, for your sake, Montell. And also, I'mma invest in penny stocks on the New York Stock Exchange with a few promising companies that pay pretty good dividends." She assured him in a phone conversation they had afterwards. This was two days from the evening that Tiffany was over.

Montell said to Verena, "Also, look, sweetheart, the business I really need you to take care of most, is especially so with my mother. I want the both of you to come together on certain matters of importance, and do things together, that only y'all two would hold control over. I want you two to get acquainted with one another, so as to have y'all form a sisterhood for the betterment of the relationship you and I are developing."

"I can do this. It's not a problem. If this is what you want. So be it. Be it so." She seemed to flow in a poetic way with her words.

***

After Montell gave Verena all of his mother's contact information, the two ladies began to talk and get to know of each other in a beautiful way. Other than this, Montell's mother was in no need of anything financially from the money the scheme made. He had already paid off his mom's home she and the step-father lived in, and had also bought her a new car. So, his mother was good in this regard. Gifts from Verena to her and through Verena from him, would work well to bring those two closer.

Once Verena told Montell about the car she was intent on buying and of the color of it, he fantasized, of the two of them riding in style, down the Las Vegas strip, or down one of the popular boulevards in Los Angeles, to watch the sun set by the beach and witness the stars coming out at night. The two of them would be among high society and mingle in excitement. *The world was now theirs to have*, thought Montell, that is, if they wanted it, and desired to be somebody in it.

The car of Verena's choice was the newest model Cadillac CTS V-Sport. The base price tag was $59,995. Verena went on ahead and bought the ride by placing a deposit of $20,000 down on one through the account she had with her mother as co-owner of their shop. What that really meant was that the car and all other purchases through the account was legitimate transactions that would clean the money from the tax scheme.

Montell felt sure through it all, the money moves Verena made on their behalf would definitely lock in his future with her. Or so he thought. And that future would be held together for all times sake.

Part Two

Chapter 25

Nine Months Later...

A new year rolled around and this brought about a new beginning. Another chance to scam again. Since the scheme from before paid off so well, Verena had it in her intentions to help Montell do the same shit all over again for the tax season upon them. Montell's words resonated with her, *"There's nothing like the second time around,"* so he said. He and Verena repeated the process like before. She provided another list of inmate names and personal information, and also, supplied a new cellphone. The money was made too easy for her to pass up. Greed took over. Women love cash more than they love anything else. It brings out the devil in them.

"So, you ready to pop this shit off again this year?" Montell said in a casual conversation they had one night. This was the second week in February.

"And you know I am! You got everything you need, don't you? I'm hooked now. I'm locked in."

"Of course, I got what I need. And I like your energy."

"Well, there you go. I'm in it to win it. I love money, Montell. It's not like I need to tell you this. It's pretty fuckin' obvious."

"I like the sound of that too. You make me feel special when you talk that shit to me like I like to hear you talk."

"The feeling is mutual."

At least for now, she thought.

"And so you'll know, the second ride itself, like the first, should be a piece of cake. Sweet as bear meat. Tasty as virgin pussy. Also, this COVID-19 shit may open up different schemes we could work to get more money. The government talking about things getting shut down and shit like a recession or some sort, and potential bailouts could happen. Stimulus money, so to speak," he uttered.

"I'm aware. I've been tuned in. Gotta make a few adjustments at the prison in preparation for what's to come. I got a lot of responsibilities ahead of me."

At the time, the Corona virus spiked and caused the pandemic. New scams were created in addition to the income tax scam. This was the unemployment fraud and PPP loan manipulation. There were totally different names and information printed out with 200 additional to be processed. Verena figured that the more information she provided, the more money they could make, which was true, for the most part. But Montell believed that maybe she'd lost sight of the fact that it was a hustle, not a guarantee.

He began to believe he may had created a fucking monster in her, and an uncontrollable beast in how she now pressed him to do more work. Was it possible that greed took total control of her? That a female demon was rising from the stacks of income tax claims being fraudulently filed? This could've been the situation. Montell would soon find out.

"The list of clients me and my guys used for the first rodeo, we not gonna use those anymore. I'm hoping you done either transferred a lot of them niggaz to a different prison, that their names won't draw any kind of red flags moving forward, or they'd been released from custody already. But for the few that remain here at the prison, I know it's best to completely disregarded them. So, you didn't include any of the old names in the new list, did you?"

"No sir. I did not. You got totally different names on your new list." "Good. So I'mma get going ASAP."

"You do that."

His advice to Verena was very specific on the issue. He encouraged her to conduct the business at hand.

"But look, the best way to take with our clients from last year, is to get rid of them. No matter how long it take. You gotta see to it that most of them be transferred. It's not a good thing to let any pattern or consistency of fake filings occur from one location, around the same time, going to one place, in the event that the IRS was to ever investigate. You'll never know if you're under investigation. So, it's better to clean up ahead of time. Because those bastards very good at all they do and is known to find out even the smallest level of fake claims. But our shit was jam up. We did 'em right."

"I trust in what you're saying. And I'll do what's necessary."

The reality of the situation was, when the IRS wants you, they'll come for you. So, it's always best to stay off their radar. Think about it, it was the IRS that had the ability to bring down the infamous and mighty Al Capone and put him away in prison. It also was they—the IRS—that brought down Montell and his crew too. So, who were *they*—Montell and Verena—for IRS to not bring down, had they forced their hand to do so, behind an outrageous number of fraudulent claims coming their way from one place? Exactly.

The fact remained that, although they processed the claims at an "A-plus" level, they were still vulnerable to the point of being discovered and investigated. Their work could still be compromised. The masterminds of the scheme, had to continue being concealed at all cost. They appeared to be safe. At least so far.

***

The timing was ripe at least this was how Montell felt for Verena and him, to get into some form of intimate activities. Since he gained the utmost trust and respect from her, not to mention that he also was the one to help her get all the free money she now had.

There is no way the bitch could tell me no with what I want now, he thought.

Montell felt he was most qualified of all, to be the guy in position to get some form of sexual pleasure from the supposedly celibate and conceited Verena. He figured his down payment and dues had already been paid, and that they only needed to make it happen. Although much had happened that spoke for him about his character and commitment in wanting to be with her on a deeper level, this too was part of it; in his mind. The being intimate part.

The first episode of sexual action came roughly two months from the day Verena picked up the money from Eric for the second round of claims filed this year.

"Look, Montell, I know and understand you're a man, and sex is vital to your overall wellbeing. But I'mma only let you play in me with your fingers. Nothing more right now. A five-minute finger-fuck is all. Besides, I always get affectionate when I'm being finger-fucked. And I want you to put your trigger finger in me and make that *'come here'* motion with it. That feels so good to me. But, back to what I was saying. This all the time I'mma give you. So, you gotta deal with it," she stated. *"You can stall him to the best of your abilities. But, don't deny him, if push ever came to shove."*

Verena had become enamored with the feeling of being fondled dating back to her adolescent years when she and Tiffany use to touch and play inside one another. This carried over to their years as teens. Then, along came somebody for Tiffany, and along came a boyfriend in high school for Verena. He replaced Tiffany with his fingers and with his *ding-a-ling.* Once enrolled into college, she found love and affection again in another female friend; Bethany Harris.

"So, the only thing you willing to let me do now is finger-fuck you? And you gonna give me a hand job with it, right?"

"Mm-Hmm! And if a hand job gotta be added, I'll do that too. You want that or you don't? But that's it. Okay," she let him know.

"Shit, anything better than nothing. Now let's get to it."

They both worked one another and made each other cum, and cum hard.

Shit, I need to come up with a way to break her out of this nervous shit she's going through. All this is new to her I see. But what more could I expect so soon, he thought.

Montell anticipated this, and he felt that in due time, Verena would begin to develop ways of getting comfortable, so as to be persuaded to continue on with doing some of the things he wanted to do. Like more finger fucks and hand jobs.

***

Montell and Verena had gotten really intimate one weekend day. A Saturday it was. While in her office on most weekends when she showed to work, the two would behave themselves like always, by having conversations on a few interesting topics of the day, or about something they may have had on their minds to discuss. Nonetheless, they'd reached a point where they had gotten more bold with actions and behavior. At any time before this, they wouldn't dare make an attempt to get loose in the way like it had became. Things like him palming her ass-cheeks how he wanted to, him wrapping his arms around her and they tongue kissing in an intense and passionate way; so on and so forth. Montell had also began to rub on her breasts. He would also lean inward and lick the top area where her cleavage showed.

He said to her, "Verena, trust me, I know it's a serious role we gotta take on, and I also know it's in my favor to play the part. It's only right that everything stay secret about the personal dealings we got going on. This our secret. Just like

145

those secrets you and your girl Tiffany keep close between each other."

"Oh, you wanna hit me with that one, huh," she said and smiled at him.

"I paid attention to all you done said."

"I see! That's a good thing."

"It was necessary. Because for the most part, people who look on at us in a certain type of way, may get the wrong impression and think that it's impossible for a nigga in the prison system, to have the type of appeal about themselves like I got, to entice or even seduce a woman of high caliber and authority like you are. It's as if to say that women like you, may not want love or affection."

Or ain't so naive as a female, to a real nigga, one that's well-kept and an intelligent dude., he thought.

"You doing really good. Just keep up the good work. And we'll see how far this can go."

"I'mma definitely do that," he came back with. "But for the record, it don't matter how high up the ladder of power and control that a female may be. The bottom line is that y'all bitches still women at the end of the day. And y'all got strong urges and desires to be loved, appreciated, and yeah, fucked real good from time-to-time. So, I get all that."

"You know how to read between the, don't you."

"That's one of my best qualities," he let out. "And as it appears, you was just the same as many other females, who met a man in a rough situation at one point or another, and found yourself in the same position, getting lucky and finding a diamond in the rough."

She pursed her lips and smirked as she thought over his insightful remark. "That's true. Most women are the same and want the same. Especially as it applies to a man. For the most part." They talked more about what they wanted to have in life.

With them, all they needed to continue doing was, being sure no signs of their business was exposed in the eyes or the mind of anyone else and maintain control of emotions. Nothing more.

Chapter 26

Weeks Later...

Montell finally was able to get the pussy. It was on a Saturday a usual day Verena would appear at work to be sure all was running smoothly. He'd pressed her really hard. She finally was willing to give in. He would never forget this day.

Verena had on this gray colored fleece sweatsuit that had her alma mater embroidered on the front. It was tight fitting and formed to the proportions of her sexy body. She had always maintained a banging figure. Montell had gotten an instant erection at the very sight of her big titties and ass she flaunted provocatively.

There was a supply storage closet in her office where stationary material was kept, and she needed him to straighten things up inside. It had been a while since he'd done so, ever since the day of the finger-fuck and hand job. She stood from behind her desk and led the way as he slowly strutted behind her. Dude had a smile on his face from ear-to-ear. It appeared more sinister than a motherfucker if anything else.

As they stepped within the small space, Montell eased closely upon her in a seductive way and poked her square between the crack of her ass with his hard on.

"Montell," she cooed in role-play. "Boy! You better stop that," she cried out playfully. In all actuality, this bitch was ready to fuck. She knew what Montell's dick looked like and how hard he could nut. She wanted now to have him hit it with his average sized but thick and wide rounded manhood. She liked the way he was built in the manhood department.

"You got a dick like the porn star guy, Mr. Marcus, you know that," Verena told Montell while giving him a hand job now to prime up and smiling.

"Oh, I do? And yo freaked out ass keep up with porn flicks, I see," he responded with an even larger smile. "So, me and Ol' Jesse Spencer built alike in the manhood suite?"

Verena giggled, because she wouldn't had never thought Montell knew Mr. Marcus's government name. "Yes!"

All the video calls, intimate conversations, the hand job, and the phone sex between the two leading to the day came to this one big moment where the both of them was in the closet to themselves and having enough time to get it in.

"I'm ready for this shit, Verena. Ready like never before," he said.

"Oh, you is?" Her girly girl side now on display. She spoke informally.

The only responsibility of a day like this for her was to be sure and keep check on the radio traffic, in the event the *Warden,* may was needed for some reason or another, or had to take a "10-21" Which is a phone call. Luckily for them, or Montell, should be said there was no need for her, nor was she called for by phone.

They both kept in mind that there was only a fifteen-to-twenty-minute window where no radio traffic would go on, since visitation was going. And, they had to do all they was intent on doing in that time frame, or nothing at all could happen.

So, without wasting a second, Montell popped it off by tongue kissing her and ravishing her neck and breast area with wet kisses. He cuffed on her ass cheeks and kissed her more passionately as she did the same to him. Verena reached down into his pants again and stroked on his manhood until it was rock hard; fully erect and damn near threatening to bust from its place of hiding.

"I belong to you, Montell. Because you provided. And I'm willfully admitting this for now, that I'm all yours. But not until you get free, that is," she confessed. Rather this was a lie or the truth, Verena said it. "You gotta get out first. But for now, we're just business partners. And I'm gonna let you get one off every now and then. Okay. But don't get too comfortable or carried away," she declared.

"If it ever gets to the point where he's pressuring you to fuck him... you need to do it. And that's simply on the strength of us now not knowing what the nigga could potentially be capable of." Eric's words come to mind again.

"Verena, I ain't tryna hear none of that future romantic bullshit you talkin' 'bout! I'm a nigga that wanna fuck!" he responded. "Right here, right now, on the spot, in this moment. Not when I get free! Fuck all that shit!"

The nigga felt that the more pressure he put on her, that eventually, she would give in. So, he put up the work necessary to get the pussy. Montell was one horny-ass nigga.

As he pressed, the thought flashed through his mind, *I gotta get some type of sexual pleasure from this bitch. Something gotta give. Right now! After all, I'm trusting this bitch with all my money, and I also gave her a lot of it. She's gotta give me a good dick suck or a shot of pussy or something!*

Montell felt he'd put in too much work only to end up with nothing sexually like he really wanted. This couldn't happen. A hand job and a finger-fuck wasn't enough.

***

Still situated in the closet, Verena seemed to beg Montell to not take advantage of her. Not to blackmail her. "Montell, please baby, please, I'm asking you, don't take my kindness for my weakness, okay. And don't take the fact that I'm a woman who happens to be weak for love and affection, the wrong way. Don't take any of it for granted," she begged and essentially admitted to everything he had already assumed anyway.

"Sweetie, take a good look into my eyes. I care about you. And I won't ever do no low down and dirty shit like that to you, or anyone else for that matter. I ain't that type of nigga. I got an old school protocol I follow. If you true to the game, then the game will be true to you," Montell told her in a very confident way.

"You promise me on that?" she sheepishly asked.

"I promise you on that, with my life sweetie. On God. Look at the things I done did already to prove myself," he further said.

"Yeah, you're right. You passed the test" she said as her resistance waned and she began to give in. "But look, I know all too well how far an inmate would take things in order to be involved with a female staff member."

He smiled. He refused to entertain her comment about an inmate and simply looked on at her without saying a word.

She continued. "I also know that, inmates, almost always, find ways to put a blackmail into the mix, if the female staff member don't comply with the wishes they are told to do," she added.

"That's not me, Verena. Now I cut the bullshit. We wasting time." Truth was, Verena was responsible for firing many staff members who'd gotten caught up with inmates. This was part of her job.

Montell was sure, that at no time before, had Verena ever thought she would one day be personally involved with one of the very same inmates she was warden over. Truth is, there was nothing that could force Montell to expose the reality of all they had, to no one else outside the know already. He'd found love and benefits with Verena. Or so he wanted to believe.

"This what I want you to know, Verena. I'm the type of nigga, who would never violate the bond that we got. But right no wall I want, is some pussy!" dude stated.

He was sure in his mind that they would get into all the other shit later down the line. But in the moment, he was ready to get his rocks off. For real this time.

Verena continued in her efforts to have him only play in the pussy as the time before. But this was only due to the high level of nervousness she still had. He panted seductively and began to sweet-talk her more, in his efforts to get her into feeling the same way he felt about the situation.

"Sweetie, please don't do me like this," he said. "Can I have a sample of it? Just let me put the head in, will you? I'll be good if only I'm able to do that. I promise to be easy and not take up too much of our time," he said.

Dude tried to further persuade her. Montell took it a step more in his attempt to appease. "All I ask is that you not do me like this. We done come too far and have taken too many risks than what we doing now, for us not to be together like this. It's nothing compared to the other stuff. You got this on lock. It's you who controls who comes through the doors of your office. Remember?" he reminded her and gave a boost of confidence.

She took everything he said into consideration. Finally, she gave in to the whims of his persistence. Montell's talk game paid off. Or was it Eric's instructions?

"I'mma do this, okay. But your ass better not get carried away from this day onward."

"I promise, I won't, sweetheart."

Verena began to loosen the drawstring to her sweatpants and untied the bow that held her cherry colored thong around her waist. She let her pants and thong drop to the floor and stood wide legged and pigeon-toed in her Nike Air Max 95' sneakers. She then reached into her bra, and brought out a condom, presenting it to Montell.

I know damn well this bitch ain't been playing hard to get all this fucking time! What the fuck type of games this bitch playing? he thought.

He put on the rubber and they got to it like no other at this point. He penetrated deep from the back and went to work.

***

Verena knew that once he'd gotten a whiff of the pussy this day, there was no turning him back from that point, from the yearnings and desires he became aroused by. He was hungrier than the werewolf of London! The man's amorous appetite was on high. Atop that, Verena revealed her deepest thoughts on the best way possible to relate with him on the issue of sex. This was after it was over.

"I knew it would come to this one day between us, Montell. I had to simply convince myself that everything would be okay and move myself to the point of going ahead and doing this long before your release. I thought over your situation and how long it's been since you last had sex. So, here I am. And finally, you got who you wanted and you got what you wanted," she said shyly as she shrugged her shoulders.

He was so eager to get the pussy. This nigga didn't last but a good three minutes at best. It was over and done with just that fast. He was too *geeked*. His sexual charge was beyond the normal, and his load had been built up for ages it seemed. Once reaching the point of his climax, his super-soaker pistol shot off every which way, once yanking off the condom. He was full of it.

This did seem to calm him down a bit, and relieved the frustrations he was going through. But, that wouldn't last for long. Things were only to last until the next time they had felt the need to get their freak on, and that he began to dictate in mind would not be too far away from the first time Verena had given him a shot of the pussy.

***

Two Months Later...

Time passed and more progress was made from the day they finally fucked. And yet again, similar to the moment before, in the same format, they was back at it. If Montell had to pick and choose, he would definitely say that the second time around was the best. This is so because, people seem to always bring up similar instances about "that first high," or "popping the cherry of a virgin," being so amazing. They seem to always chase after one of the two for seconds.

Verena's confidence boosted. She became thorough with things now.

"You got me all into it again, Montell. Those feelings of sexual satisfaction is back. I went so long without sex, now, I can't think of going again without it," she made him aware.

Maybe this was so because Montell had showed and proved himself capable of holding his weight and keeping his mouth closed about everything to everyone but Eric. But he hadn't uttered not a word to anyone about them fucking. Not even to his main man, Eric. But shit, he was getting the pussy too. So…

The mood caused them to get all the way loose with things for round two. And so, as they stood in the closet, he and Verena got ass-hole naked. Montell did a good job at working the kinks from her. She was somewhat scared. But not much. He motivated her to get with the fucking program.

"Verena, yo ass gotta loosen the fuck up and live a little!" And, to his surprise, the bitch had done more than expected. She became what he wasn't ready for her to become.

"So, you want me to loosen up and live a little, huh. Okay. I can do that. I can *definitely* do that," she declared, then got with the program on him.

Of course, she was the one who brought the rubber. And, she was the one who also had her mind situated on the idea she would show some feminine spunk and lead the way.

"I'm a take charge type of girl, Montell, as you may know. And if I'm gonna keep giving you the pussy, I can't keep being so scared and shit, you know what I mean."

"Fuckin' right, I do!"

At taking notice of this new side of her he hadn't seen before, Montell thought, *well okay then Verena! You go girl! With your bad self. Yeah. Do your thing.*

Verena held him in a tight embrace. She locked lips with his. Montell then laid down on the floor and let his dick stand straight up at a ninety-degree position. His honey-complexioned professional freak bitch then straddled him, squatting down on the dick spread eagle.

What the fuck! This bitch done gotten good at this shit, I see! I guess she been practicing on the low all the while or doing something to help better her skills.

In actuality, Verena's demeanor displayed a bit of flare, like it's always been there, but only needed someone to bring it out of her. Montell never seen her get so loose and behave so naughty as she had that day. He liked it. She'd turned into a bad girl. It appeared she'd found a touch of her days as a youth. Maybe of those once enjoyed in high school or college.

Flashes of her sensual side and sexual frustrations collided with one another, as it appeared she wanted to reveal a pleasing and mature version of herself. This was possibly so, to prove she could be professional in the presence of the one she found intimacy with, yet, she made a way to let those truly stimulated desires express themselves without her being taken simply a freak at best and a hopeless romantic at heart. Someone who she'd previously confessed to being.

Verena tried her absolute best to conceal both, the "freak" she really was and that "hopeless romantic," she'd turned out to be, but failed so miserably at it.

"A nigga 'bout to beat this pussy up! You hear me! I'm 'bout to beat it up! Wait till it's my turn to get on top. It's been a long time, too. So don't pick at me if I nut too fast again, okay," he said in his own funny way.

Verena smiled at him and thought over all he'd just said.

"Two months ain't a long time, Montell," she responded, shaking her head slowly and holding her smile.

As she rode him, they eventually switch positions. He took control from there. Montell began to hit shorty from the back, long stroking hard with each thrust, causing her to cry out, "Ooh God! Maurice! This dick is good to me, baby. Pound harder for me, will you. Hit it harder! Get it like you want to, motherfucker you!" She motivated him on.

He did as told and pleased her how she wanted it. Their business lasted longer this time. Maybe ten minutes. He reached his climax point. What he'd done to prevent being premature was, he'd beat his dick the night before, as he wanted to last longer to satisfy his own desires.

"Oh shit, Verena! I'm 'bout to nut, girl," he let out now busting one.

He oozed his load into the condom while still penetrated deep inside the walls of her love-box. He finally withdrew and removed the condom, then placed it into the thick swath of toilet tissue she rolled off and handed to him. She then wiped herself clean with a sanitation napkin she had on hand and pulled up her thong, tied it back around her waist, then her sweatpants, and quickly adjusted herself to the appearance of "the warden," there at work on the weekend. She rushed to the restroom to get rid of the tissue and all that was wrapped inside it.

She returned to the closet to be sure Montell was properly dressed and told him to clean the entire area. There was a need to eliminate any smell of sex from the air. He did as she asked and deodorized the closet, using heavy air freshener. After this, he pecked her on the lips and cheeks before leaving to head back to the dorm. They both exchanged smiles of pleasure.

As Montell strutted down the sidewalk, he strode his hands down the freshly pressed prison garb he was draped in, so to straighten out any wrinkles that may have formed. He was really feeling himself behind the good sex he had not long been involved in. How good it was for the both of them. This probably was the best fucking he'd had in the past two decades. It was all that to Montell. Without doubt it was. Maybe it was the thrill of knowing he was fucking *the warden*, and at how he'd worked his way to that point. It took a little time and a lot of money, but nonetheless, he made it happen. This was all that mattered.

Chapter 27

Months Later...

As the days turned to weeks, weeks to months, and time passed them by, Montell's life as an imprisoned man was coming to an end. The never-ending video calls and conversations, along with phone sex and all else, had really helped he and Verena reached a special space in what they had. It seemed that they had been in a relationship for years. The vibe raised no eyebrows or made them suspicious in and around administration. The control of their emotions were in check too.

But opposite this, Montell developed this eerie feeling of "guilt," since he was responsible for causing Verena to become sexually re-invigorated, and having the hots for a nice fat dick to be penetrated between her legs, inside of her. It was as if her sex life had literally been brought back from the dead. Her desire to have her pussy pounded had laid dormant for several years. And at the point of the cat being let free from the hat and Pandora's Box busting wide open, once her love juices started to flow again as spring water from the fountain of youth, she couldn't get enough of the action. She wanted more of it. And Montell, had it all on reserve for her too. So did Eric.

Montell knew from years before, for all things that occur more than twice, the third time, shall be the "charm." This turned out to be the occasion for Verena and him. They were in a similar situation as the times before in her office on a

Saturday in the supply closet and horny as ever. The only difference was that the season had changed. Nothing more.

He said to her, "I'm almost a free man, sweetie. Only five months to go, and the timing couldn't have been better for us now."

"I know you can't wait to get free, can you?"

"Hell nawl, I can't! We'll be able to have more of each other then. You'll have *all* of me, and I'll have *all* of you, I hope," he worded.

"Um-hmm. I bet."

Verena saw to it that Montell ate the meals she also ate herself, and all else that came along with what she provided. He was able to do what the fuck he wanted to, it seemed, and he was pleased with the fact. Who the fuck could tell this nigga anything? He was fucking the warden! And in certain instances, Montell ran the compound. Because inmates know more about the prison than the officers do. He was a man on top his game, and a nigga who had a lady of power, rule, and authority in his life. Montell maintained his composure though as the inmate he was, and didn't get too arrogant. He never developed the *big head*. His position was like what a real nigga's position was supposed to be, as he had grind so hard to build himself up to become. *I'm the motherfucking man!* he fancied himself this way in thought.

***

The third sexual escapade for the two was to be more of a farewell episode than anything. Verena seemed to want to be a naughty little bitch this time, as all bouts of nervousness had gone out the window. She took the initiative to demonstrate what she was now made of.

While lounging in the office, sipping on cups of coffee and munching on home baked chocolate chip cookies she treated, the free-spirited attitude she long struggled to suppress, broken free and went into its element.

Without Montell noticing, she suddenly embraced him with so much energy and passion that it took the man by total surprise. Verena began to tongue kiss him in a possessed type of way. It was as if this bitch would need an exorcism or something to the effect! The bitch had gotten crazy.

She aggressively urged Montell, "Give me the dick, Daddy!" she demanded. He had to take a good look into her eyes and saw that she may had turned into a "nymphomaniac, or possibly reverted to one. Either or, "I'm ready to fuck, Maurice! Right now, too!" was what she stated emphatically. This was definitely clear. "Now come on. Let's go to the closet," she dictated.

"I'm right behind you, sweetie," he responded.

No sooner had she passed the doorway point of the supply closet, she quickly pulled down the sweatpants she religiously dressed in on weekends and untied the powder blue G-string she had on underneath. This bitch was eager and anticipated getting to the action. Montell was handed a condom and ordered then and there to get naked ASAP and put the rubber on his dick.

"I'm so ready for it today, baby! You better know, I am!" she declared with high energy.

"Shit, me too!" he responded with a smile and began to strip down.

Part of Montell's grooming was to shave all his body hair—under arms, chest, back and pelvic area—as he had performed this ritual of his the night before their secret meeting was to take place. The muscle tones and chisels of his body glistened from baby oil.

"Ooh Maurice! I love this body you got, baby." She excitedly stated and placed her hands on his chest as she began to caress slowly and passionately.

"This body of mine is all yours too, sweetie," he replied with confidence. "It belongs exclusively to you, boo."

"Hurry and put that damn condom on, won't you! That's all you need to be doing. I want it bad, baby! I want it Maurice!" she stated in order that he speed up the pace.

He hurried as fast as he could to put on the jimmy hat and laid down on the floor. Montell assumed she wanted the pleasure of starting the party off how she saw fit and taking charge like always, being she wanted it so bad. He thought right. Verena then jumped on the dick and began to ride in reverse-cowgirl. It was a five minute interval

Montell was then allowed to pile-drive deep in the pussy as if it had never been beat down like this before. He was intent on giving the pussy the business this day. He'd gotten so charged up to the point of rushing to put the rubber on as she demanded, that in his speediness to dive head long into the juice-box, a terrible mishap occurred that he was unmindful of to stop and fix. Once they got going, it was too late to stop and get it together. So, he simply kept going and didn't give a damn about nothing else.

As he reached his climax, Verena palmed both his ass-cheeks tightly and held him firmly locked in position. He was still deep inside her. She held the man hostage the entire thirty to forty-five seconds it took to blast his load and drain his nut sack. It never dawned on him that a mishap had occurred until the moment he withdrew from her.

Indeed, Montell knew the accident had to be explained to her regardless of anything he may have came up with in his mind to say to her, being that the situation was serious and had to be spoke on. If only it could be explained in words the look of absolute despair that came across her face the moment he let her know what happened.

"Verena. We got a problem, sweetie," he said casually, like it really wasn't an issue. "It's a problem baby," he added. He then pointed to what the situation was.

She took notice and became hysterical at this point. "Oh no! What the fuck! Oh my God! How did this happen, Montell?" she questioned in a high-pitched whisper.

"We rushed it, sweetie. I was moving too fast and didn't pay attention."

"Oh my God! No! Lord, no!" she screamed. She repeated herself over and over and over again, as if chanting *Hail Mary's* or something to the effect in prayer

Montell stood motionless with his hands on his hips and his dick limply dangling, leaving the condom crinkled and loosely fitting. He kept quiet and dared not utter a word once putting the issue out there.

The rubber busted. The mistake was that he hadn't pinched the tip to create enough space for his load to be placed in. Shit happens. This was the way of the world.

The majority of his cum was still inside her. There was no way she was able to contract her internal muscles to strain out what he shot up in her. Rather inadvertently done so or not, all Montell knew, he'd shot up her club. He'd plastered the walls of her womb.

"I gotta get this mess outta me!" She said, now frantically working to get the baby-making liquid from her body.

After several failed attempts, she gave up the fight and yanked the condom from Montell's manhood with two fingers and a thumb, wiped him down with a sanitation napkin, and then, went to flush everything down the toilet in the office restroom.

Once properly dressed again, she pecked him on the lips like always and said to him, "Don't be worried about nothing. Everything will be fine, because I don't think I could get pregnant. So just go back to the dorm for now, and I will see you come Monday."

Before leaving, he mentioned that, "I'll do anything you need me to do, Verena," allowing his obsequious manners to hold an effect on her thoughts.

Later that evening, Montell tried calling and texting her to find out exactly how she was feeling. But she ignored everything and apparently had turned off her phone. There was no desire to talk. Her mood was not well, to say the least.

***

Three Weeks Later . . .
The full truth behind the mishap came to the light. Verena took a leave of absence from work, and Montell only had the chance to exchange text messages once throughout the time. She admitted that indeed, "I'm pregnant, Montell. I found out not long ago. This was the reason for the time off. I went to the doctor."

His fucking heart sank to his knees. "I'm tryna figure out why I don't feel so well about this," he let out.

The news made him feel as though the prison chaplain had told him he had death in the family. Like someone close to him had passed. This was the feeling he had at first. But then, it all changed. For the better.

"My time away was the necessary space for me to begin the process of a thorough soul search, a mission I'd went on to gain spiritual advice and whatnot," she informed Montell. "But once I'm back at work and into the groove of things, I'mma make it my business to personally let you know face-to-face that, indeed, I had contemplated having an abortion. But my better judgment and reasoning spoke against this diabolical thing. I know without doubt that the good Lord would certainly punish me, had I went on to terminate my baby, God's creation of human life, that is," she believed. "I was raised Christian."

Verena was indoctrinated with a strong pro-life mentality as a staunch Evangelical Christian and a Georgia Republican Party member. Her mother and aunt also had a lot to say on this and urged her to get away from such demonic and crazy notions.

Montell's opinion was that, "Verena, personally, I believe you had gotten so caught up in your career and on the professional side of things, that you long lost desire or interest to have kids before becoming pregnant. That's just my take."

He was sure that at some point along the way, her urge to do so was re-installed, based on the fact that Tiffany had the type of family life she so badly wanted, and would do anything to have.

Montell discovered these facts in hindsight, through the endless conversations they would have after the fact of where Verena would relate to him about things like this. Although indirectly.

She told him, "The only way I know how to express my true desires, affections, and yearnings, is to slowly reveal them in this way, indirectly. So, don't be offended if I act funny or isolate myself from you and everyone else, okay."

"I won't. And I understand."

At the moment she made him aware of her decision to keep the baby, and that they both needed to find a way to establish a stronger bond, Montell was sure to internalize everything related to him, and was afforded the chance to give her his advice of how he felt.

"I'm just glad you keeping the baby. And I thank you. Because I don't got no kids, and do want some. I'm almost forty. I want a family of my own."

"As you already know, so do I."

Everything Montell mentioned to her in this conversation went hand-in-hand with all she had been leaning towards to begin with. So, all there was left to do was to go about things according to the goals and plans they already had laid out.

The money that belonged to her and Montell played a crucial part in answering the personal questions she evidently had in her own mind. And her action plan was to go on and submit her resignation papers after four years as Warden to the Commissioner of the Department of Corrections, the man who appointed her to be warden.

Within her resignation, Verena would make it known that the reasons for her intended exit was due to multiple changes in focus, in career choices, and in profession. She also stated she needed to care for her elderly mother who required assistance. Her leaving the career in corrections occurred exactly four months short of Montell's release date.

Verena was sure to leave him a farewell gift. It was the latest Apple iPhone he now had. She also blessed him with a few other trinkets to go along with the device, to help *"carry you through to your release date."*

Montell was fortunate. *"I'm very blessed,"* he often told people. *"I'm winning. And winning in a major way!"*

***

Months Later...

Montell was four months short of being released. He was serious about seeing to it that all he and Verena scammed for would be situated and secured. The trust was established on many levels. He felt certain she would take care of business and manage their money well.

The two had come a long way together as undercover business partners and had taken extreme risks to get the type of cash they now had. They couldn't afford such a fall from grace to happen at the snap of a finger and then lose it all just like that. Indeed, Montell learned valuable lessons from his past mistakes, and couldn't repeat those errors twice. Least he'd be the damned fool that some would want to see him become over the better decision-maker he found himself now to be.

Verena had a lot of questions for Montell leading up to this point, and he didn't mind answering. His thing was, if a woman questions you like she had, it's something about you she's interested in. Maybe he was right.

Chapter 28

As the end of Montell's incarceration approached and Verena's career in corrections closed out, a strong sense of relief was brought over her. With the things she desired most.

She said to Montell, "I feel I was blessed to have a handsome and good man in my life in you. We got a baby on the way. And we certainly financially situated for the future. I got a positive outlook on life, Montell. And we can now pursue the finer things that life has to offer. This the plan to do together. Okay," she stated.

He responded to her, "I was fortunate to plant my seed in the womb of a woman who got high standards, intellect, and capabilities. I'm the lucky one."

Verena's stature as a woman was a benefit to him. She had worth and knew her worth. She was also desirable and far beyond that of the females he'd dealt with in the past. As far as money was of a concern, he never worried too much about that, since his hustle and drive had always been on point. This aspect of his life presented no problem.

In the last conversation they had, Montell said to Verena, "My future," he had foreseen, "has began to truly take shape and establish a foundation. Something to capitalize from. Life beyond prison, I mean. All that is left is for my release date to come faster than the pace things is moving. I'm so fucking anxious to get out! And I done already visualized you pulling up to get me in the new Cadillac you got, and you dressed in a cherry red Vera Wang dress, cream colored

Christian Louboutin Red Bottom heels, and clutching a Gucci designer briefcase, packed with the cash we done scammed for. My black-ass wanna don one of those expensive fedora hats, a solid white silk button down shirt by Versace slightly exposing my chest and waiting to be embraced by you at the exit gate. That's what I want," he told her. This was a dream he had. A *"pipe dream"* maybe. Not hardly a vision.

Verena was his "wife to be," and, she had their unborn child in her womb. They both had a promising life ahead of them. She now had a home that was long paid for, and had an add on to it, with some of the money Montell provided. This gave him a little say-so with her. She utilized some of the money from the schemes to pay for added luxuries to the estate, an elegant gate, and a thorough landscaping job. They also had a few legitimate businesses to capitalize from.

And Montell had cash and jewels secretly stashed, awaiting him. What more could a man in his position ask for? His life was a happy one to be enjoyed after all.

"Verena, something I wanna tell you. At the very beginning of this prison bid, I never thought for once that what appeared to be a rough road I had to travel would actually turn out to be a blessing in disguise. This was my first time getting locked up. With that being said, I end this Chapter of my life by realizing to myself that, when the government knocked us off, me and my crew, no doubt they did set us back a few years and a hundred steps. But it eventually caused a transition on my behalf, into a situation where a nigga now flying high in a better life; and into bigger and better things; with nothing holding me back to alter or cause me to fall off. That's what I wanted to say," he once said to her before everything fell apart.

How seriously blinded could a nigga be when all the signs and other evidence was there to draw a conclusion about? The writing was on the wall. All Montell had to do was pay close attention. But he didn't see it. That's another story for another day.

As with all endings, one door closes while another one opens to create new beginnings. This would conclude one reality, so as to establish another. Montell couldn't wait to explore it.

***

The official countdown to freedom was certainly on and popping for Montell, as he had less than thirty days left in prison, then would be released to society once again. He would be completed of both Federal and State time behind the white-collar crimes he and his homies were convicted of years ago. However, all is well that ends well.

Montell anxiously anticipated the moment he was to walk out the front gate of the prison, the very place where he'd managed to seduce Verena, and where he'd spent the last nearly three years of incarceration. To this end, it happened to be the very same place that he'd put together his schemes to hit for all the money he now had, his biggest take so far. The Corona virus pandemic was a gift and a curse to many. Everyone was effected by it.

But, as with any story, a lot of them don't end well. Verena killed the contact between them. He had no idea what was going on. A phone call was made to his next close homie, Jamie, since Eric seemed to have disappeared too.

"Yo Jamie, I don't know what the fuck is up, bro! When was the last time you and Rod seen Eric?"

"We ain't laid eyes on that nigga in a minute. Ain't heard from him either. Why, what's up?" he responded.

"Shit! What's up is that we done made these moves and got all that bread, and now, I can't get hold of him or my bitch! Something ain't right, bro."

"Oh fuck, Mo! You for real?"

"Fuck yeah, I'm for real! And on top of that, all the dough we licked for, the bitch was holding for me! That was everything I had. I need that to fall back on," he lied.

"I know that's right. But in the meantime, what you need me and Rod to do?"

"Shit! I'mma need y'all niggaz, to keep looking for that nigga E, and find out what really going on on the low."

"Gotcha, my nigga. We gonna do that," Jamie gave his word on. The phone conversation lasted maybe a minute more. Montell was too pissed off to keep talking with anybody.

But the same place from where Montell had been hindered and deprived of enjoying life, liberty, and the pursuit of happiness, it turned out to yet offer him prosperity and fast money to use in helping him get back on his feet. And he would be damned if he was gonna let it all just be taken from him like that by the same people who he got the paper with. Although through illegal means, he still had it.

Once free, being above it all and through it all, he had no obligations of parole, probation, nor any other attached sanctions by the state of Georgia which would slow his progress. At least none he readily knew of, if his plea agreement was properly understood by him at the time.

Montell's efforts at being accepted into a transitional center, halfway house, was to no avail, due to the 'high risk nature of potentially breaching security.' He was denied the opportunity to participate in such program. No biggie. It was all good. He still maintained his sanity, his psychological acuteness, and kept his physical and spiritual qualities intact; his four most overlooked blessings, and no trauma happened to him at no time throughout his bid.

"Montell, I'm sorry. The parole board decided to not grant you this opportunity. They want you to max out your time. Also, you won't be able to go to a halfway house either. They say you didn't qualify. Good luck," his case manager

counselor Mrs. Duncan had said to him. Her words played in his mind again.He was crushed at the defeat.

Okay! No problem. Since they don't wanna let a nigga get out early or go to a halfway house, I'mma make them bitches pay for this shit, he thought behind the denial. This was before he put the scam together.

At the point of Verena resigning from the D.O.C. due to her many reasons—all related to previous activities she had to keep secret as best possible—Montell managed to still remain as the administrative aide/orderly, on work detail he'd held for a couple of years, even under the new warden who'd arrived. Warden Martin Burrow was the typical early fifties white guy, who felt the need to exercise his authority and rule over the predominant black populated prison a little more than necessary.

Tiffany was in the process of moving on to something else in the area she specialized, as disagreements and reserves about the personality and style of the new warden didn't go over too well for her. Simply put, she didn't like dude. He went about running things awkwardly. Doing too much basically. Besides, Verena did mention on many occasions, the both of them would eventually start their own business, and Tiffany would be the C.O.O. of the enterprise that was to be created. However, not only had Verena cut all contact with Montell, for whatever her reasons turned out to be, she'd temporarily communicated with Tiffany as well. But it was Montell who was the one to get the worst end of Verena's scorn and disappearing act.

I can't even begin to think of what the problem is why Verena has not gotten in touch with me, and why she's changed all information I got to reach her, Montell often thought after the fact.

Verena changed everything; phone numbers, discontinued email accounts, terminated payments to the post office box, and everything. To Montell, it seemed as if "she'd fallen from the face of the earth!" He was left with the only sense of hope there was to hold on to, that all was well on her end, and the baby was good. Verena simply needed more time to herself away from everyone, he thought.

Even though Montell had no more contact with Verena or anything to let him know her whereabouts, he still felt comfortable all was good. And hopefully, every dime of the money he'd scammed for and depended on was safe and secured. But the perception Montell held verses the reality of what she showed, was very far and distant in between.

***

At the point of Montell being able to finally make his exit out the front gate, he had plans to spread his arms wide and scream to the heavens above. "Free at last, free at last! Thank God Almighty, I'm free at last!" He mentioned to everybody who would listen that this was what he was going to do.

Montell's plan was to go to his mother's house, get the money and jewelry he had situated there, then, head straight to ATL from that point, looking to relax, and rest his head in the comfort of the home Verena supposedly was to also buy from the money he'd produced. It had been her job she was to utilize, and her credentials, to get the house approved through the bank.

With the six small business start-ups operating and doing good, according to the last reports Montell got from Verena before she changed the log-in information, shutting him out, he again felt there should be no problem adjusting to society as a reformed ex-con turned businessman/investor. But being that Verena had hauled ass and now nowhere to be found, giving him her ass to kiss before he was to be set free, it may become hard for him again, as hard times loomed if any loss happened—if Verena doesn't show back up.

Each time he contacted the bank and attempted to know what the hell was going on, why can't he log into his account? The bank people didn't provide any information.

Montell knew something wasn't right. To be perfectly honest, Montell didn't know what the bitch Verena was up to or what she had going on.

"I'm left completely lost, dumbfounded about it all, bro," he said to Jamie. "And, to add insult to injury, this nigga Eric, the main nigga I trusted, ain't no longer able to be contacted himself, for whatever reasons he's got. This makes shit even more suspicious, since Eric and Verena did communicate and met on a few occasions for the money exchange."

Neither Jamie nor Roderick were able to reach him either. *What the fuck really going on with Eric?* Montell thought over. He had no idea whatsoever what the deal really was. He was pissed off and determined to know what was up, and soon.

***

Not long before his discharge from prison, Tiffany made it her business to let Montell know she would be leaving the job for another the next week after he's released. She'd been hired by Home Depot at headquarters to do office work there, much like she had at the prison. Since Verena *flim-flam* her at the last minute about the so-called business they were to create, Tiffany knew it was important to keep a stable job that paid well and had good benefits.

On Montell's last day in prison, he pulled Tiffany to the side to talk for a moment, as he wanted her to explain to him, "What the fuck was going on? And where in the hell was Verena, my *supposedly* friend, and your friend?"

"Tiffany," he called her by first name. Enough with formalities. The bullshitting was done. She gave him a look of shock as she seemed surprised he would become so bold and address her the way he did. But she was okay with it at this point. She'd already known more than Montell may had ever thought. "Please tell me where the hell is Verena? And what the fuck going on?" he demanded.

"Montell I'm gonna just tell you in an up front and direct type of way, alright. Because if you must know, I already know. But look. You may as well just forget all about Verena and any plans you thought you had with her, okay. Forget about that damn woman, man! Forget about the money. And forget about everything else you felt there was between you two, won't you," she cold hearted responded.

"What the fuck you mean by that, Tiffany?" His confusion about the situation forced him to ask.

"I tell you what. Once I get back from lunch, I'll let you know everything that needed to be known. And in fact, I'll just show you. So be ready to handle the truth, okay," she said to him.

"Oh, I promise you, I will be," he replied, and they went on.

The lunch hour break passed and Montell raced his black-ass back to detail, anxious as ever to be made known on all the shit his girl Verena had going on.

"Okay, we're back. The Warden ain't returned yet, and we the only ones here for the time being. So ain't nothing stopping you from spilling your guts and telling me all you know," dude Montell eagerly stated.

The area was clear from the ears of anyone else other than Tiffany and Montell for the brief moment, and she was free to talk. She pushed the door up close enough but didn't close it all the way, in the event the warden or any other staff members were to walk in, they wouldn't suspect anything out the ordinary between the two. There was a small trash can exposed behind the door Montell could easily give a good excuse on as to why the door was up close as it was.

Suddenly, Montell was taken totally by surprise. Tiffany grabbed him by the shoulders, pulled him inward, then wrapped her arms around his waist and quickly pecked him on the lips, then lightly on the neck. She made it her business to physically express the long pinned up lust and desire for him she had. It couldn't be held any longer. Her yearnings imploded.

She then grabbed both his hands and guided them all over and around that nice, plumped ass of hers, to make Montell questioned himself, *how good could the sex with Tiffany truly be?*

Tiffany finally began to talk on the issue, "You see Montell, had you took half the time to pay me a little attention like you gave to Verena, and put some of that focus towards this right here," she gestured with her hand up and down her body, "you would've had a more true and loyal woman by your side, the type of woman who would have certainly looked out for you and kept your best interest at heart. But you didn't. You chose to do it your way, which turned out to be not so good for you in the end."

"How you know about all that?" he asked

"Montell, are you serious right now dude? Are you really being serious with me? So, you mean to tell me, as smart and as conscience of a man that you are, you hadn't paid any attention to the storm that was brewing right before your very eyes? A 'hell' and a 'fire' storm that you helped to create, by being the 'Mastermind who made her rich,' in her own words. You failed big time in not taking notice of the monster and money-hungry bitch you brought to life with that scam of yours you had going on," she mentioned.

"I'm gonna ask you once more Tiffany. How do you know all this?" he wanted to know. Montell smiled in his efforts to disguise the anger he felt. Tiffany detected the emotions in his voice. She continued.

"Verena is my 'best friend' for crying out loud Montell. Not only that, but she is also my only friend I find myself extremely close to. Do you understand what that mean?" she spat.

Montell continued to keep silent and didn't say a word. He let Tiffany do all the talking.

"It means, we hold the deepest darkest secrets of each other's lives. That's what it mean, dude. Verena shares everything with me... *everything* sir. Hell, she even gave me some of the money you hit for from the tax thing, dickhead!" Tiffany momentarily went into her college girl element in attitude and words. "I know exactly how she got the money to pay for that nice-ass Cadillac she now drive. I know how she got the money to pay for those expensive jewels and all those other material possessions she owned. I also know about the two hundred thousand plus dollars you gave her out of what you scored for, so she could pay down on the new home she's began buying, and the other money she used to start those businesses with. I believe it was more like seven hundred thousand or more, if you count the second score as well." She made Montell realistically aware she had knowledge of everything.

"Now, I know damn well Verena ain't told you about all that, has she?" he responded.

"I know damn well she did too," Tiffany retorted. She then jarred her head and spoke more. "I'm starting to think a little different about you now, Montell. How many times do I gotta repeat myself for you?" Tiffany stated sarcastically with a cold stare and squinted eyes, as she held him closely again. She actually felt sorry for Montell, being she knew Verena had played him for an absolute fool.

"Well, since you already know much as you do, you mind telling me what the fuck going on?" Montell conceded then demanded.

"I can't tell you what's up with her at the present moment and time, because I'm not so sure myself. I haven't talked to Verena in quite a few weeks, possibly months even. We did text though. But, what I am going to tell you is this. Verena is a very calculated and time taking individual in how she goes about doing things. She has always been this way. If she can't find a way to manipulate a situation to be of benefit to her, then, she won't bother getting involved. But if it's a will, it's a way with her. She's on board. The problem Verena have is she has to be in total control of every damn thing. She is a control freak, Montell. By all means, I tell you. I needed to free myself from under the dominant rule and power she had over me. I had gotten so sick and tired of working for her and allowing her the pleasure to control me the way she has since our childhood. I got tired of it Montell. I really did," she let him know.

Chapter 29

Tiffany happened to put a look of disgust and disappointment on her face as she revealed the dirty side of nature her best friend's character carried along with it. Montell would have never thought for one time Verena would dare share anything like she had with anyone. How wrong was he. Tiffany continued.

"I bet you don't even think I know anything about the two of you having sex either, do you?" she joked. "All was right there in the office in that supply closet," she stated and pointed towards the location she spoke of. "I know about Verena being pregnant and everything too, Montell. But here's the thing *you sir* really need to know," she had stopped short of completing all she intended to say and told Montell she'll get to the worst and most hurtful part in a minute. "I need time for you to be able to digest all the appetizers before we get to the main course, the absolute about all that's really going on," Tiffany related. "I wanna show you something, okay Montell. But you got to promise me you won't flip the hell out and lose control of yourself. Besides, your fine-ass on the verge of being a free man anyway. So, ain't no need to get all in your feelings and emotions over this. And for God's sake, please don't beat me up by releasing your anger on me with those boxing skills you got, or go off and punch holes in the walls, because you can't handle this," she joked and laughed at the humor of her own words.

Montell had to do so himself.

Tiffany pulled out her smartphone and hit the gallery app to access the photos. The pictures she began to show Montell had literally began to fuck him up mentally. To a great degree. He couldn't believe all he saw with his very own eyes. And no, none of the pictures were photo-shopped. He was one angry dude. But no matter what, he had to keep his word with Tiffany and maintain his cool. It was Tiffany who was the sincerest person he felt was left in his corner on the affair, and the only one who had his best interest at heart about the situation.

The pictures showed a smiling "happy-go-lucky" Verena, all hugged up with the "most trusted dude of Montell's crew," Eric. The two were together down at a beach resort in the Virgin Islands. As Tiffany began to scroll through the photos, they appeared to get more explicit. Then, they'd reached the ones which showed a fully naked Verena, all snuggled and wrapped tightly with a fully naked Eric himself, as they kissed and posed for the camera in front of a full-length body mirror.

Eric's dick was fully erect and extended to a rock-hard peak. It's not truly known why Verena would send Tiffany such personal photos as those, but she may have felt comfortable doing so, being they were best friends, and had in times past seen each other's body far too many moments to count. It was okay to have done so, and it had to be the truth, since Tiffany accepted them, and kept them stored in her phone for whatever her reasons was, if not only to be messy by showing them to Montell.

DAMN! I can't lie. Eric's dick is bigger than mine. I wouldn't have expected it to be a fact from a light-skinned dude, in comparison to a dark-skinned dude as I am. But what the fuck. If it was dick Verena wanted or was after, then I could've given it to her myself. But I guess it was the "over-sized" dick she desired, along with the money she got me for. Oh well. What the fuck! Montell had thought.

The photos showed Verena holding onto Eric's dick like she had won an "Oscar Award" or some other grand symbol of achievement. The bitch even had the nerve to make a personal video of herself, a homemade video sucking on Eric's dick and having him stuff as much as possible down her throat, as he massaged her tonsils with the head of his beef sausage while being pleased.

"Yo Tiffany! What the fuck that video all about?" he asked about the oral sex recording.

"I guess Verena wanted to show and prove to me she finally learned how to provide pleasure to a man mouthwise. It was a little thing of ours in high school. Verena never knew how to do all of that until I showed her. We used to practice on cucumbers and bananas," Tiffany explained and laughed at the same time.

"I knew females could be weird as hell in a way. But you two are *crazy*," Montell said and continued to look on in surprise.

Verena showed off with Eric for Tiffany in the photos and videos, as she felt her friend would continue to safeguard all of her "deepest and darkest secrets." Verena would have never fathomed Tiffany, of all people, being the one who would breach the trust and loyalty, then expose her business to anyone. Montell to be included.

The most troubling and hurtful part of the pictures was the ones which showed the sonogram images of the unborns Verena carried in her womb. There's twins. Montell readily assumed the seeds planted were his. But then again, once it dawned upon him all that was truly going on, he finally began to have reservations about that being a fact.

The final photos showed Eric and Verena hugged in the nude, with him situated behind her and both arms looped around her waist palming her belly as it bulged.

***

Montell was completely crushed as a man behind the sight of *his lady* with his best friend and him now having full knowledge of it all. He felt like a fool. A total idiot, for not being able to recognize everything when it began developing and unfolding, at the expense of his folly. If it was to be anyone who would instantly transformed from a humble and civil minded person, directly to being crazy and psychedelic in a sense of a killer, this person could easily be Montell from that day forward.

The bitch that Verena had turned into, caused Montell to be someone he had never imagined he'd all of a sudden become: a mad-man, and really wanted to fuck somebody up! Verena and Eric had become enemy number one. Montell was double-crossed by his most trusted *friends*—his lady Verena, and, his fucking homie, Eric. What the fuck was really going on? What was really real? And what wasn't? Montell was at a loss for words and mentally gone for the most part.

Tiffany spoke out more, "Montell, I know what I'm about to tell you may add more insult to injury. But I have to tell you. I can't relate to you one part without telling you the other. So go ahead and brace yourself. Okay," she warned.

"Damn! There's more?"

"Hell yeah. But look. Before that last time you and Verena had sex, the time the condom broke, she had already been fucking somebody else."

"Apparently so! Obviously, Eric, right?" he put out there to save a little face.

"Well, I'm not here to lie to you, my guy. I won't do that to you. You done suffered enough. And more lies will only make a bad situation worse. But anyway, look. Verena was already three weeks pregnant at the time y'all last did the nasty. The baby she carrying is not yours, man. Excuse me, let me correct that. The *babies* she's carrying, aren't yours. They're Eric's. As you now are aware," she reluctantly revealed with a bit of caution.

Montell put both his hands atop his head and his jaw dropped, leaving his mouth agape. "Damn! Twins?" he let out in astonishment. "Why couldn't that have been me she's pregnant by? As bad as I want children."

Tiffany didn't respond. She simply kissed Montell for the last time that day. Because she knew, he was to be set free the morning after, and, she would not see him any longer. At least not in prison.

"Yep. She got twins on the way. Sorry for you, Montell. I really am," she acknowledged.

"I now know you fucks with me, Tiffany. I know you mean well. And now, I'm kicking my own self in the ass for overlooking you, for her! And this how they do me! What the fuck!"

"Just be easy. Everything gonna be alright. A'ight. Be cool," she advised.

"The first chance I get, I'mma fuck both them bitches up! I'mma make 'em regret every crossing me. I swear to God on my grandma's grave I am!"

"Just be cool, man."

Montell gave her his word he would keep in touch once he was out. She gave him her phone number and other contacts to do so with. They ended the conversation and went about their separate ways. Montell went back to the dorm to vent and blow off some steam. He would not return to detail anymore.

***

The much-anticipated day for Montell arrived. He could hardly rest from eagerness to get free. He gave the roommate Harold and the friend snoop, each a cellphone a piece. They all were in his cell talking and awaiting the 8:00 A.M. count to clear and the guards to come get him to be processed out.

He said to them both, "Y'all niggaz be cool up in this bitch when I go, okay. Y'all day coming soon too. And be sure to keep in touch. That's why I'm leaving y'all these phones to do so with. A'ight!" He never factory reset neither device. This was a costly mistake. One he and others would pay for later down the line.

"For sho', Mo! We gonna hold it down and keep our motion going," said Snoop first. "Thank you too, my nigga."

"No doubt."

"Yeah, Montell. I really appreciate the love, fam. And you was a really cool roommate to have. A rare breed of a young nigga. You gonna do great things once you out. Mark my words," Harold expressed.

Not long after the farewell pow wow of the trio, Montell was escorted to the intake area and changed out of clothes. He was finally released. The weather was nice and sunny. It was the second week of July and the summertime heat and energy were in full effect. The original plan of his was to have Verena pick him up in the new Cadillac he came up with the money for her to buy. But that particular plan had not gone too well. It was his sister, Ciara, and her boyfriend, Demar, who drove to the prison to pick him up. They returned to Albany nearly four hours later.

***

For Montell's first two weeks being out, he decided he would stay at his mother's house until he'd gotten himself together and gained some sense of balance and stability. After all, his mother's house was the place he had his money and the jewelry stashed. He immediately went to get everything within one hour of being there. He contemplated finding a job. But, Montell was not the manual labor type of nigga. And besides, he had no parole or probation. At least none to his knowledge, he thought. And wasn't in need of any money seriously. So, a job per se, was out the question.

***

Three Weeks Later...

Montell packed up and headed back to Atlanta to live, the city where he stayed prior to being arrested. Atlanta was perfect for Montell to take residence, if in fact, he decided to get back into the game and make more money on the white-collar side of things.

He began renting an apartment to live until he was to figure out how he would do things. Also, he contacted one of his ex-girlfriends, Tamron Bryce, and let her know he was a free man again. Not that she didn't already know. She knew he would come crawling back her way sooner or later. Because he wanted some pussy. And she wanted his dick. She was happy as ever to hear from him, as they hadn't talked in months.

Tamron had no problem swinging by his place to let him hit it real good from the back as he liked. But the thing was, since the last time the both of them had been together, Tamron, had taken a liking to the same-sex, and found great pleasure in being with women now, more so than with men. A confused world some might say. Nonetheless, her and Montell never experienced a dull moment whenever he did have time for her, out of the heavy rotation of females he ran through. They were to hook up in the week.

One day with being back in Atlanta, finally, Tamron came by to be with Montell. They had so much to talk over. She initiated the conversation.

"Montell. It's so much we gotta catch up on. But we definitely got time to. Just not today, really. Because it's all about you, and your being free again and here spending time with me. And you already know, I wanna fuck you, and fuck you good, like I plan to do. And I want not one, not two, but *three* orgasms of my own, before you bust a nut yourself. And you can nut all over me how you see fit too," she let out explicitly. She always told Montell *exactly* how she wanted to be fucked. He liked her dirty ass mouth. *Nasty bitch, you!* he thought behind her words.

"*Sheez, boo!* Talkin' 'bout making up for lost time! Damn!"

"Oh, most definitely, nigga! But on second thought. Instead of you nutting all over me, I want you to nut deep in my ass like you use to love doing. That's of course, once you beat down hard and deep in this pussy of mine."

"Oh really! You still on that '*not wanting to get pregnant and fuck up your figure*' shit, I see."

"You know me, don't you. And we ain't gotta worry about no pregnancy scares this way, now do we. Because, I don't want no babies, Maurice! At least not right now," she stated. "So, cum shots in my mouth, or cum shots in my ass only. Okay."

"Well, if you don't wanna be the one to have this unvaccinated nut of mine shot up in you, then somebody else gonna have to be. Because I wanna be a daddy."

"Nigga please! You better march your healthy and happy ass right on down to one of those damn sperm banks close to one of those college campus' any town USA and sell that shit to some bitch who wanna get pregnant! Not waste it! Because they paying top dollar right now. Between \$3,000 to \$5,000 a shot! And again, I ain't tryna be knocked up," she stated.

"I remember reading about something like this online not long ago before I got out. So, I researched it from there. Everything checks out about that."

"I'm sure it does," she responded with a smile.

They continued to talk a little longer before the fucking finally began. Montell ended up blowing his load deep in Tamron's ass just like she wanted him too. She was a super freak and loved to ass fuck. And was pleased each and every time she got a fat dick stuffed in her tailpipe. *My dick is like Mr. Marcus' dick! And I'mma work Tamron's ass like one of his favorite porn bitches!*

***

Montell was immediately informed by Jamie about Verena, when they finally met up. He said to him, "This is what me and Rod found out, Mo. That nigga Eric, the bitch Verena, and her momma, all moved up north together, to Princeton New Jersey to live. They bought a house there. We can't say exactly where in Princeton, because we don't know. But we do know, *Princeton*."

"Now that I think back, I do remember the bitch Verena mentioning something about having an aunt who lives there and said something about her mother always wanting to be back in close living proximity with her sibling. But I do got an address to the house in Buckhead when the bitch once lived. So, I'mma swing by there, just to be sure that the bitch has actual moved. I need to know for sure."

"Sounds like a good idea. Do what you gotta do, my nigga. Just let me know if you need my assistance with anything. That's a bet," Jamie responded.

"For sho' bro."

"For sho'."

Montell was provided Verena's address during the many times he'd messaged her as *Todd Debonair,* on Messenger and IG, and, she had no knowledge that her phone locator was activated. Ever since that day, he knew where she lived. Also, he found out additional information when he took a ride over to Eric's momma's house and getting her to talk, before she'd remembered Eric specifically told her not to mention anything about him to Montell. Under no circumstances. Eric's mother contested at first, being she knew how close the two of them once was. But then, made it her business not to be between the two, because she felt it was more to it than meets the eye, so she stayed out of it.

But, in addition to the money Verena had snaked Montell out of, she also had power of attorney rights to the lawsuit settlement her mother received from the medical malpractice claims against a doctor and the hospital the male physician worked. The payout from that totaled 1.7 million. And once the settlement had been reached, Verena's mother, Mrs. Deanne wanted badly to move away from Atlanta and head to the Garden State. Verena also handled her father's estate, in addition to the lawsuit settlement.

They took the family pet poodle, "Tiny," with them too, as life was good for Verena and Eric for the time being. But in the mind and the intent of the one who'd been hurt the most by Verena and Eric, *that bitch has hell to pay! And pay dearly they both would do for the bullshit they'd pulled!* So thought Montell. He couldn't let it go. It wasn't no way he would.

Chapter 30

Montell was with his boys, Jamie and Roderick, again. These two had definitely amplified the hustle and really began to get money. They utilized the bread from the names and the movement Montell had going on, to invest into their own scams, and they paid off. They had expanded to a greater level in activities, both legally and illegally. They'd pooled money and hit Montell off with it to get back on his feet, since they had knowledge about the bullshit Eric had done, by back door him for Verena.

The three had gotten together and went out to eat at the Cheesecake Factory to discuss a few things and formulate what they wanted to do next.

"Yo, Montell, it's real fucked up how that lame-ass nigga Eric did you, bro!" Roderick opened the door on the subject.

"Yeah, it's all good Rod. It's all good. The only thing to really piss me off about it all, was the fact how he convinced the bitch to take all the money she had. It really belonged to me. If that wouldn't have happened, I couldn't care less about the bitch! Real talk!" Montell let it be made known.

"So, it's not so much about the bitch, but more so about the *money* that got you so mad, right?" Jamie chimed in.

"Exactly, bro! Exactly. The money *and* the betrayal E had done. Because I took some serious risk and real penitentiary chances to do what I'd done from prison to help him get more money than he'd ever had in his life. And this is how I'm repaid? My own nigga gonna cross me out and run off

187

with my bitch! I'mma see that nigga again, though. I promise," Montell capped.

"That is fucked up bro. The nigga Eric got *me* pissed at the bullshit! Now that we look at it, what other type of bullshit has that clown-ass nigga done did behind our backs we don't know anything about?" Jamie stated.

"That is something to think about, yo. We all know the nigga got bitch in his blood too. So, if you get too close Montell, or become a major threat, he may run to the Feds to report you, or get the warden bitch to do so," Roderick had put the warning out there.

"Since we on the subject of muthafuckas' telling and reporting on niggaz, what's the deal with that bitch Rico?" Jamie asked

"I'mma pull that pussy up right now online," Montell said and Google *BOP.Gov* on his phone and entered Rico's name and other information. "'Rico Locus.' It says here, his bitch-ass is out in Victorville, California, at the USP there. He probably not on protective custody any longer," Montell revealed the search results.

"Which means that that lame-ass nigga can finally be touched!" spat Rod. "All we gotta do now is find a way to get in touch with some gangsta-ass niggaz up in that piece and put the lick out on that bitch! For the old and the new!" Roderick added.

"You definitely got the right game plan there, my nigga," Montell co-signed.

"Goddamn sure do," Jamie joined in.

Roderick and Jamie had brought Montell up to par on all the new ways to freak and finesse the tax scheme under the new code, and, on the subject of the many other financial scams they'd gotten good at. In the rare moment, the two of them had easily persuaded Montell to get back to doing the same line of business he'd once been a part of. He only needed to do things better for the second act. There was no way possible for Montell to have resisted the temptation to get back knee deep in the game.

His boys, Jamie and Roderick, had also given him $30,000 each to help him get going good. Montell needed the extra money to get all the necessary tools and the material to fire the hustle back up and going strong again. Not to mention the money and jewels he already had and didn't tell them anything about.

Epilogue

Montell played it smart in many ways. He had stolen several other inmates names and personal information before he got out, so as to utilize at a later date. He was to not run short on the list of "available" clients he had intentions to use. He had 1000 personal profiles. Atop of that, he still had Tiffany to depend upon if need be. She purposely placed herself in his life for whatever her reasons were. All that mattered was that she was there. He did give her a call four days after being set free. But the conversation didn't last long.

Montell only wanted to touch up on a few things with Tiffany and would use her to lead him straight to Verena in due time. Tiffany informed him of many things. She made him aware of the fact her marriage was on super-thin ice. She also told him she was in the process of retaining an lawyer to file for the divorce. She most definitely desired one.

With Montell being back in ATL, the hometown city where Tiffany lived herself, the both of them were at close proximity to one another, as times in the past when he served out his prison sentence. The lesson learned from before was for him to not overlook her anymore, as he had made this terrible mistake in choosing Verena over her. He was certainly intent on utilizing Tiffany's talents and skills, as a resource, to get far ahead and back on the "right side of the money" as opposed to the "dirty side" of it. By legitimate means, he wanted badly to correct himself in all his ill-deeds and ways of living.

Tiffany was a good woman, and Montell knew this all too well. If only he had took heed of this fact at the on-set. And had he possessed any minute level of insight to foresee into the future and know what the end-game might turn out to be, without doubt, Tiffany would have been the top pick. Not Verena. Now that he look in hindsight, he was able to know exactly why Tiffany would sit and simply shake her head at him often, as he moved about at work, in and around the office. She must had knew eventually, he would get played and pushed around like a pawn in Verena's game of "control chess."

Tiffany was too afraid of losing her job, had she made any attempt at revealing anything to Montell of all she knew, or, if the other scenario was to play itself out with her indicating she indeed had a crush on him. Verena would have fired her ass, as fast as the former President Donald Trump had fired people on "The Apprentice," or out the White House as he had throughout his tenure at the helm.

There also was a deep fear of another reality Verena held over Tiffany, if she was to ever get too sassy and out of line. Little to Tiffany's knowledge, Verena had already spilled the beans to Montell on her most deep down and darkest secret of all her secrets. Besides the fact that she took a blood-oath and vowed to never utter one word to no one, not even to *God* himself, if he was to ask her about it. She lied vehemently. Verena told Montell all about it. Each and every long detail of her "secret."

***

Years Ago...

Tiffany once experienced an emotional and psychological breakdown, associated with having went through the procedure of an abortion. She was at the tender age of sixteen at the time. A couple of years after the termination of the first pregnancy, Tiffany eventually gave birth to her daughter, Chasity her only begotten and the Goddaughter of Verena.

Chasity had never been made known of the fact of exactly who her *real* father was. She and her mother's husband, Matthew, Chastity's perceived father, had the absolute impression that he was the one to plant his seed within the womb of Tiffany. But that turned out to be so far from the truth. One thing was for certain, Tiffany knew the truth, and so did Verena. Not to mention the fact Montell now does too.

Tiffany's parents knew absolutely nothing about the abortion. She hid everything well, the pregnancy and the termination, the whole nine yards. A brief summary of Tiffany's forbidden story is this:

In the final two months of her senior year of high school, she had gotten pregnant for a second time by the same guy. She had complete determination to keep the baby she carried this time around. No matter what was said to her or who should go against her decision. She kept aloof from her parents for very good reasons. They were the ultimate religious type and held high ranked positions in the "Mega Church" they were members of. An "arrangement" was ordained years prior for Tiffany to marry the elder son of the pastor, Matthew II, who was ten years her senior. The marriage was to take place at the time she graduated, just before her entry into college there in Atlanta. That did occur and the marriage was consummated the day of the wedding.

Remember that Tiffany was already pregnant by another man. And as far as Matthew and the parents knew, the baby in her womb belonged to the son of the bishop the chief assistant to the bishop himself, Mr. Matthew Peter Long II the twenty-eight-year-old runner up to succeed his father at some point in the future.

At the time Matthew and Tiffany had their first sexual encounter, she was six weeks pregnant. So, a lie had to be thought up to convince her husband and their parents otherwise. Chasity had been born at the nine month phase as any normal pregnancy is to be. But, according to Tiffany, her daughter entered into this world nearly two months prematurely. The parents and the husband took the lie, hook, line, and sinker without questioning anything on no level. There had not been the slightest hint that dear Tiffany had perpetrated an all-out lie to save her marriage and her face before her parents and the church. She'd kept to her guns in the situation.

The Full Truth Is...

In Tiffany's freshman year of high school, she and Verena joined the female swim team together. Tiffany took a great liking to the Coach/Trainer of the team, Justin Dewayne Manderville and possessed an uncontrollable crush on the guy, who had mixed background. His father was black and his mother was Korean. Indeed, Justin was already a married man with two kids by his wife Katie, and he could not have afforded to jeopardize such livelihood by sneaking and creeping with a young high school "teeny-bopper" Tiffany was at the time.

But Justin simply could not resist the thought nor the lustful yearnings he experienced, of the young beautiful heartthrob he had the 'green light' to do whatever with, whenever he saw fit. Atop that, Tiffany was a virgin. She hadn't been penetrated at any level. And so, Justin gave in to the carnal instincts which strongly suggested he sex the hot and appealing Tiffany.

The affair they'd began was strictly based on sex. Nothing more. He impregnated her in short order and had to do something fast to conceal his dirty deeds and infidelities. He forced Tiffany to have an abortion, as he provided all the money and drove her himself to Jacksonville, Florida for the procedure to be performed. Had anything about the pregnancy leaked out, certainly, that would have spelled trouble for the child molesting bastard Justin had become, being that Tiffany was only fifteen at the time, two months shy of sixteen, and not the first to be taken advantage of by him.

Their dealings carried on for nearly three years, up until Tiffany graduated from high school. And throughout the time, Justin repeatedly maintained his way with her in many regards sexually; oral, anal, and vaginally as he released his load inside of her each time. Thankfully, Tiffany had been prescribed birth control, or else, she might had gotten pregnant more times than she had before she stop taking them.

Prior to her leaving high school, she'd gotten pregnant again, and decided to keep her baby. Unfortunately for Justin, the truth of him sexing under-aged girls on his swim team to include Tiffany had begun to be exposed little-by-little, as an investigation had been launched by the school upon one of the girls making mention of it.

He was suspended without pay, and between the time, Justin packed up his family and immediately hauled ass to live in the commonwealth state of Virginia, the state where he had family in, and, the state that housed his alma mater, Virginia Tech. He landed a job there in Virginia as a high school swim coach/trainer, of all positions.

The gavel finally came down on Justin not long after he relocated to VA. His long and "pleasant" career of socking it to little girls, and also passive gay boys, had come to a crushing and devastating end. He had gotten arrested on a 13-count indictment by both a Federal grand jury and a State judicial prosecutor. He was hit with a hundred- and fourteen-year prison sentence with sixty to be served in Federal lock up.

Tiffany's secret had remained between her and Verena, until Verena told Montell all about it. Even to the very day, Matthew, still believes Chasity is his daughter, and likewise, the daughter believes that the assistant bishop Matthew Long II is her father, and that she holds the last name and blood of a family whose brand and name rings loud all across the country in Christian religious circles, most notably, those that affluent black people adhere to and follow with their life.

Through the years, Tiffany has maintained contact with Justin. She has even gone so far as to visit him a few times, and has almost always sent him money, letters, and pictures of their daughter they have. It is guessed and might be safe to say that she is "dangerously in love" with the guy. A man who had given her her first and obviously her best sexual experience.

Rather she agrees to the fact that he had taken advantage and manipulated her into believing molestation and statutory rape, could be construed to mean "consensual" or not. Truth be told, Justin was in her life to stay, even though he stands the chance of never seeing the light of day of freedom again. She loved him dearly through it all and vowed to stay by her daughter's father's side, irregardless of who or what. She had his back, and that was all to it.

At times, she often questioned herself at how she would be able to defend herself or think of the next best lie to tell, if it ever gets out the truth of who the father of her daughter really is? Without doubt, she won't be the one to relate the ugly truth or open her mouth about a damn thing. Her lips are sealed on this deal, as they have been for twenty plus years. And, she has even threatened to "kill" Verena, in her own mind, if she ever betrayed her on what she knows pertaining to that reality. So far, all has been going according to what was told from the beginning: a fucking bold-faced lie!

To Be Continued...

Acknowledgements

First and foremost, I would like to give praise and thanks to the highest above—The Creator—for the wisdom strength and beauty, I am blessed to have. This precious gift of life has allowed me the opportunity to write and create the works I now produce. Had it not been for the beautiful struggle I've experienced and endured, there would be no compelling stories to imagine or relate. So, on the strength of that, I would like to salute all of you that are maintaining the struggle.

All Praise is due to The Most High Father-God above. May the Peace and Love be upon ALL righteous nations, groups, religions, individuals, or otherwise, regardless of affiliation, denomination, race, nationality, ethnicity, or creed.

May the peace and love be upon the true pioneers of "Realistic Urban/Street lit," "Realistic Prison Fiction," and "Realistic Fiction" period; to whom I follow the path of, for they were the first to live it and do it best. R.I.P. Iceberg Slim (1918-1992), Donald Goines (1937-1974), and Chester Himes (1909-1984)

May peace and love be upon my two beloved sons; John ("Jonesee") and Hasim ("Chief"). To my dear mother Cynthia; my father Mack Sr.; my step-fathers Elvin and Larry; and to my grandparents—R.I.P. Ada Mae and Lonnie (Pavo), and Idella and Frank Sr. To my three sisters Monica, Shemeka, and Danielle. To my brother Derrick (The youngest Boss in the city of Moultrie). To all of my nieces and nephews—my sister's and brother's children. To each and every family member I have (The Trimble, Allen,

Solomon, Thomas, Stewart, and otherwise family members I have), from statewide-to-nationwide to international. I want to especially shout out my three cousins, Willie James C. ("Poosie"), Quentin Matthew D. ("Q-Dawg"), and Tremaine Antonio T. ("Big Nat").

Truth be told, had it not been for you three guys introducing me to the streets, the dope game, and my experiencing the struggle with you all, I'd never known nothing of how to survive in the hood, or how to hustle and win. REAL TALK! It is because of you that my mind and eyes became opened to the power of the hustle and a solid grind.

May love and peace be extended upon both the mothers and the families of my two sons (The Johnson family and the Law family).

May the peace and love be upon all my family members and friends that are no longer physically here. R.I.P. To the hood Prince and street legend of Moultrie, Mr. Devorest Shanzell Cokley aka "Deek" or "Knowledge." R.I.P. Willie Lawrence Bender Jr aka "Lil Willie" or "Chill Will." R.I.P. to everyone else. There's simply too many to list. I love you and dearly miss you all.

May peace and love be upon each and every person, group, organization, or otherwise, that has shown me love or supported me in some way, shape, form, or fashion throughout my doing this prison sentence or for the purchase of this book. I thank you.

Shout out to everyone that knows me from citywide-to-statewide-to-nationwide. I AM HERE! I HAVE FINALLY ARRIVED! I HAVE FINALLY BECAME! With the use of my mind and my pen, I am empowered and divinely rehabilitated through the art of writing. It's my ONLY SALVATION! I shall never be forgotten nor overlooked. FACTS!

Shout out to my hood of "Forest Hill" in Southeast Moultrie (Roosevelt—"Big Knuckie," Big Meechie, and

Bonny—"BL," what's good); Bloomsdale in Levittown, Pennsylvania; The *Badlandz in North Philly;* and "Brown Sub" in Miami, Florida. Stand up!

I'm sure that I covered everyone, but for whatever reason I missed you, please don't be offended. I simply forgot. It's human error. I'll be sure to get you in the next work.

May peace and love be upon all of the real individuals that reside in the "Belly Of The Beast," whether Fed, State, or County, both male and female. If you real, you real.

Last but absolutely not least. I purposely saved some of the best for this part. May peace and a deep love be extended to a couple of very special and dear friends of mine, Miss Trenekia Nicole Williams aka "Nikki," and Ms. Latoya D. Lane aka "LaToya Styles." I love you Nikki and thank you for everything. I value and appreciate your companionship, Toya, as the best has yet to come. I promise not to allow any of this acquaintance of ours go in vain. May God be my witness.

Forever, I Am
—Prince

About The Author

PRINCE, is a writer of gritty, raw, dark, and suspenseful contemporary urban/street crime fiction. The works of his, embody American society and African-American culture, as is, in the way that it is. Nothing less. Nothing more. The characters he creates, are realistic in nature, in all of their wiles and ways. The style of writing Prince has developed, speaks for itself. You're drawn in the more and more you read, until you're locked there; with one way in and no way out. In a word to describe his skills within the craft: it's **LETHAL.**

Prince, vehemently declares at every opportunity that, *"WRITING, IS HIS ONLY SALVATION!"* He stands firmly on business with this.

The works he's released thus far in addition to this, is the popular **BLOODLINE OF A SAVAGE** series (three installments to date); **THESE VICIOUS STREETS** series (three installments to date); and **RELENTLESS GOON** series; (three installments to date) to name a few. More captivating stories are on the way.

Prince is currently hard at work on his next installment of the story you've just read. Look forward to new releases from him soon. He highly encourages feedback and engaging conversation about his books in general and the writing industry as a whole. You may contact him at the following:

PRINCE A. TAUHID #952058
MACON STATE PRISON
P.O. BOX 426
OGLETHORPE, GEORGIA 31068
iamprinceforever3000@gmail.com

The Pen Is Mightier Than The Pistol
EMBRACE WRITING!

Lock Down Publications and Ca$h Presents
Assisted Publishing Packages

Due to an increase in the price of services we have increased our prices. The prices below reflect the price increase as of 11/1/24.

BASIC PACKAGE **$699** Editing Cover Design Formatting	**UPGRADED PACKAGE** **$1000** Typing Editing Cover Design Formatting Upload eBooks to Amazon Upload Paperback to Amazon
ADVANCE PACKAGE **$1,400** Typing Editing (line editing/content) Cover Design Formatting Copyright Registration Proofreading Upload eBooks to Amazon Upload Paperback to Amazon	**LDP SUPREME PACKAGE** **$1,700** Typing Editing (line editing/content) Cover Design Formatting Copyright Registration Proofreading Set up Amazon Account Upload eBooks to Amazon Upload Paperback to Amazon Advertise on LDP's Amazon and Facebook Page

***
Other services available upon request.
Additional charges may apply

Lock Down Publications
P.O. Box 944
Stockbridge, GA 30281-9998
Phone: 470 303-9761
Email: lockdownpublications@gmail.com

Submission Guideline

Submit the first three chapters of your completed manuscript to ldpsubmissions@gmail.com. In the subject line add **Your Book's Title**. The manuscript must be in a Word Doc file and sent as an attachment. Document should be in Times New Roman, double spaced, and in size 12 font. Also, provide your synopsis and full contact information. If sending multiple submissions, they must each be in a separate email.

Have a story but no way to send it electronically? You can still submit to LDP/Ca$h Presents. Send in the first three chapters, written or typed, of your completed manuscript to:

LDP: Submissions Dept
P.O. Box 944
Stockbridge, GA 30281-9998

DO NOT send original manuscript. Must be a duplicate.
Provide your synopsis and a cover letter containing your full contact information.

Thanks for considering LDP and Ca$h Presents.

NEW RELEASES

BLOODLINE OF A SAVAGE 1-3
THESE VICIOUS STREETS 1-3
RELENTLESS GOON 1-3
BY PRINCE A. TAUHID

THE BUTTERFLY MAFIA 1-3
BY FUMIYA PAYNE

A THUG'S STREET PRINCESS 1&2
BY MEESHA

CITY OF SMOKE 3
BY MOLOTTI

GET IT IN SLUGS 1 &2
BY B. STALL

STANDING ON HER BUSINESS 1&2
BY DG SANTANA

STEPPERS 1,2&3
THE REAL BADDIES OF CHI-RAQ
BY KING RIO

THE LANE 1&2
BY KEN-KEN SPENCE

THUG OF SPADES 1&2
LOVE IN THE TRENCHES 2
CORNER BOYS
BY COREY ROBINSON

TIL DEATH 3
BY ARYANNA

THE BIRTH OF A GANGSTER 4
BY DELMONT PLAYER

PRODUCT OF THE STREETS 1-3
BY DEMOND "MONEY" ANDERSON

NO TIME FOR ERROR
BY KEESE

MONEY HUNGRY DEMONS 1-2
BY TRANAY ADAMS

HUB CITY MENACE 1-3
BY J. WHITE

A THUGGISH PASSION 1&2
LAND OF DA HOOLIGANZ 1-4
KILLAZ ON STANDBY 1&2
BY IRA B.

FO'EVA ROLLIN 1&2
BY ASSA RAYMOND BAKER

THE LEVEL UP 1&3
BY LUXURY KING

Coming Soon from Lock Down Publications/Ca$h Presents

IF YOU CROSS ME ONCE 6
ANGEL V
By Anthony Fields

A THUGS STREET PRINCESS 3
By Meesha

CORNER BOYS 2
By Corey Robinson

THA TAKEOVER
By Keith Chandler

BETRAYAL OF A G 2
By Ray Vinci

SAVAGE FAMILY EMPIRE 1&2
SOULLESS GOON 1,2&3
THE DIRTY SIDE OF MONEY 1,2&3
By Prince

FOR MY ENEMY'S SAKE
AMBITIONS OF A SLIDER
FRESH OFF DA PORCH
By IRA B.

THE TRUCKLOAD 1-4
TIPPIN' THE SCALES 1-3
BAD BITCHES WIT GUNZ 3
PROBLEM SOLVED 2
By Christopher "Diesel" Hornezes

Available Now

RESTRAINING ORDER 1 & 2
By **CA$H & Coffee**

LOVE KNOWS NO BOUNDARIES 1-3
By **Coffee**

RAISED AS A GOON I, II, III & IV
BRED BY THE SLUMS I, II, III
BLAST FOR ME I & II
ROTTEN TO THE CORE I II III
A BRONX TALE I, II, III
DUFFLE BAG CARTEL I II III IV V VI
HEARTLESS GOON I II III IV V
A SAVAGE DOPEBOY I II
DRUG LORDS I II III
CUTTHROAT MAFIA I II
KING OF THE TRENCHES
By **Ghost**

LAY IT DOWN I & II
LAST OF A DYING BREED I II
BLOOD STAINS OF A SHOTTA I & II III
By **Jamaica**

LOYAL TO THE GAME I II III
LIFE OF SIN I, II III
By **TJ & Jelissa**

IF LOVING HIM IS WRONG...I & II
LOVE ME EVEN WHEN IT HURTS I II III
By **Jelissa**

PUSH IT TO THE LIMIT
By **Bre' Hayes**

THE DIRTY SIDE OF MONEY | PRINCE

BLOODY COMMAS I & II
SKI MASK CARTEL I, II & III
KING OF NEW YORK I II, III IV V
RISE TO POWER I II III
COKE KINGS I II III IV V
BORN HEARTLESS I II III IV
KING OF THE TRAP I II
By **T.J. Edwards**

WHEN THE STREETS CLAP BACK I & II III
THE HEART OF A SAVAGE I II III IV
MONEY MAFIA I II
LOYAL TO THE SOIL I II III
By **Jibril Williams**

A DISTINGUISHED THUG STOLE MY HEART I II & III
LOVE SHOULDN'T HURT I II III IV
RENEGADE BOYS 1-4
PAID IN KARMA 1-3
SAVAGE STORMS 1-3
AN UNFORESEEN LOVE 1-3
BABY, I'M WINTERTIME COLD 1-3
A THUG'S STREET PRINCESS 1&2
By **Meesha**

A GANGSTER'S CODE 1-3
A GANGSTER'S SYN 1-3
THE SAVAGE LIFE 1-3
CHAINED TO THE STREETS 1-3
BLOOD ON THE MONEY 1-3
A GANGSTA'S PAIN 1-3
BEAUTIFUL LIES AND UGLY TRUTHS
CHURCH IN THESE STREETS
By **J-Blunt**

CUM FOR ME 1-8
An LDP Erotica Collaboration

THE DIRTY SIDE OF MONEY | PRINCE

BLOOD OF A BOSS 1-5
SHADOWS OF THE GAME
TRAP BASTARD
By **Askari**

THE STREETS BLEED MURDER 1-3
THE HEART OF A GANGSTA 1-3
By **Jerry Jackson**

WHEN A GOOD GIRL GOES BAD
By **Adrienne**

THE COST OF LOYALTY 1-3
By **Kweli**

BRIDE OF A HUSTLA 1-3
THE FETTI GIRLS 1-3
CORRUPTED BY A GANGSTA 1-4
BLINDED BY HIS LOVE
THE PRICE YOU PAY FOR LOVE 1-3
DOPE GIRL MAGIC 1-3
By **Destiny Skai**

A KINGPIN'S AMBITION
A KINGPIN'S AMBITION II
I MURDER FOR THE DOUGH
By **Ambitious**

TRUE SAVAGE 1-7
DOPE BOY MAGIC 1-3
MIDNIGHT CARTEL 1-3
CITY OF KINGZ 1&2
NIGHTMARE ON SILENT AVE
THE PLUG OF LIL MEXICO 1&2
CLASSIC CITY
By **Chris Green**

THE DIRTY SIDE OF MONEY | PRINCE

A GANGSTER'S REVENGE 1-4
THE BOSS MAN'S DAUGHTERS 1-5
A SAVAGE LOVE 1&2
BAE BELONGS TO ME 1&2
A HUSTLER'S DECEIT 1-3
WHAT BAD BITCHES DO 1-3
SOUL OF A MONSTER 1-3
KILL ZONE
A DOPE BOY'S QUEEN 1-3
TIL DEATH 1-3
IMMA DIE BOUT MINE 1-6
DYING FOR LIKES
By **Aryanna**

A DOPEBOY'S PRAYER
By **Eddie "Wolf" Lee**

THE KING CARTEL 1-3
By **Frank Gresham**

THESE NIGGAS AIN'T LOYAL 1-3
By **Nikki Tee**

GANGSTA SHYT 1-3
By **CATO**

THE ULTIMATE BETRAYAL
By **Phoenix**

BOSS'N UP 1-3
By **Royal Nicole**

I LOVE YOU TO DEATH
By **Destiny J**

I RIDE FOR MY HITTA
I STILL RIDE FOR MY HITTA
By **Misty Holt**

THE DIRTY SIDE OF MONEY | PRINCE

LOVE & CHASIN' PAPER
By **Qay Crockett**

TO DIE IN VAIN
SINS OF A HUSTLA
By **ASAD**

BROOKLYN HUSTLAZ
By **Boogsy Morina**

BROOKLYN ON LOCK 1 & 2
By **Sonovia**

GANGSTA CITY
By **Teddy Duke**

A DRUG KING AND HIS DIAMOND 1-3
A DOPEMAN'S RICHES
HER MAN, MINE'S TOO 1&2
CASH MONEY HO'S
THE WIFEY I USED TO BE 1&2
PRETTY GIRLS DO NASTY THINGS
By **Nicole Goosby**

LIPSTICK KILLAH 1-3
CRIME OF PASSION 1-3
FRIEND OR FOE 1-3
By **Mimi**

TRAPHOUSE KING 1-3
KINGPIN KILLAZ 1-3
STREET KINGS 1&2
PAID IN BLOOD 1&2
CARTEL KILLAZ 1-3
DOPE GODS 1&2
By **Hood Rich**

THE STREETS ARE CALLING
By **Duquie Wilson**

STEADY MOBBN' 1-3
THE STREETS STAINED MY SOUL 1-3
By **Marcellus Allen**

WHO SHOT YA 1-3
SON OF A DOPE FIEND 1-4
HEAVEN GOT A GHETTO 1&2
SKI MASK MONEY 1&2
By **Renta**

GORILLAZ IN THE BAY 1-4
TEARS OF A GANGSTA 1/&2
3X KRAZY 1&2
STRAIGHT BEAST MODE 1&2
By **DE'KARI**

TRIGGADALE 1-3
MURDA WAS THE CASE 1-3
By **Elijah R. Freeman**

SLAUGHTER GANG 1-3
RUTHLESS HEART 1-3
By **Willie Slaughter**

GOD BLESS THE TRAPPERS 1-3
THESE SCANDALOUS STREETS 1-3
FEAR MY GANGSTA 1-5
THESE STREETS DON'T LOVE NOBODY 1-2
BURY ME A G 1-5
A GANGSTA'S EMPIRE 1-4
THE DOPEMAN'S BODYGAURD 1&2
THE REALEST KILLAZ 1-3
THE LAST OF THE OGS 1-3
By **Tranay Adams**

MARRIED TO A BOSS 1-3
By **Destiny Skai & Chris Green**

KINGZ OF THE GAME 1-7
CRIME BOSS 1-4
By **Playa Ray**

FUK SHYT
By **Blakk Diamond**

DON'T F#CK WITH MY HEART 1&2
By **Linnea**

ADDICTED TO THE DRAMA 1-3
IN THE ARM OF HIS BOSS
By **Jamila**

LOYALTY AIN'T PROMISED 1&2
By **Keith Williams**

YAYO 1-4
A SHOOTER'S AMBITION 1&2
BRED IN THE GAME
By **S. Allen**

TRAP GOD 1-3
RICH $AVAGE 1-3
MONEY IN THE GRAVE 1-3
CARTEL MONEY 1&2
By **Martell Troublesome Bolden**

FOREVER GANGSTA 1&2
GLOCKS ON SATIN SHEETS 1&2
By **Adrian Dulan**

TOE TAGZ 1-4
LEVELS TO THIS SHYT 1&2
IT'S JUST ME AND YOU
By **Ah'Million**

THE DIRTY SIDE OF MONEY | PRINCE

KINGPIN DREAMS 1-3
RAN OFF ON DA PLUG
By **Paper Boi Rari**

THE STREETS MADE ME 1-3
By **Larry D. Wright**

CONFESSIONS OF A GANGSTA 1-4
CONFESSIONS OF A JACKBOY 1-3
CONFESSIONS OF A HITMAN
CONFESSIONS OF A DOPE BOY
By **Nicholas Lock**

I'M NOTHING WITHOUT HIS LOVE
SINS OF A THUG
TO THE THUG I LOVED BEFORE
A GANGSTA SAVED XMAS
IN A HUSTLER I TRUST
By **Monet Dragun**

QUIET MONEY 1-3
THUG LIFE 1-3
EXTENDED CLIP 1&2
A GANGSTA'S PARADISE
By **Trai'Quan**

CAUGHT UP IN THE LIFE 1-3
THE STREETS NEVER LET GO 1-3
By **Robert Baptiste**

NEW TO THE GAME 1-3
MONEY, MURDER & MEMORIES 1-3
By **Malik D. Rice**

CREAM 2-3
THE STREETS WILL TALK
By **Yolanda Moore**

THE STREETS WILL NEVER CLOSE 1-3
By **K'ajji**

LIFE OF A SAVAGE 1-4
A GANGSTA'S QUR'AN 1-4
MURDA SEASON 1-3
GANGLAND CARTEL 1-3
CHI'RAQ GANGSTAS 1-4
KILLERS ON ELM STREET 1-3
JACK BOYZ N DA BRONX 1-3
A DOPEBOY'S DREAM 1-3
JACK BOYS VS DOPE BOYS 1-3
COKE GIRLZ
COKE BOYS
SOSA GANG 1&2
BRONX SAVAGES
BODYMORE KINGPINS
BLOOD OF A GOON
By **Romell Tukes**

CONCRETE KILLA 1-3
VICIOUS LOYALTY 1-3
BLOODY MONEY BAGS
By **Kingpen**

THE ULTIMATE SACRIFICE 1-6
KHADIFI
IF YOU CROSS ME ONCE 1-3
ANGEL 1-4
IN THE BLINK OF AN EYE
By **Anthony Fields**

THE LIFE OF A HOOD STAR
By **Ca$h & Rashia Wilson**

NIGHTMARES OF A HUSTLA 1-3
BLOOD AND GAMES 1&2
By **King Dream**

214

GHOST MOB
By **Stilloan Robinson**

HARD AND RUTHLESS 1&2
MOB TOWN 251
THE BILLIONAIRE BENTLEYS 1-3
REAL G'S MOVE IN SILENCE
By **Von Diesel**

MOB TIES 1-7
SOUL OF A HUSTLER, HEART OF A KILLER 1-3
GORILLAZ IN THE TRENCHES
OOPS CRY TOO 1&2
THE DAUGHTER OF A CARTEL BOSS
By **SayNoMore**

BODYMORE MURDERLAND 1-3
THE BIRTH OF A GANGSTER 1-4
By **Delmont Player**

FOR THE LOVE OF A BOSS 1&2
By **C. D. Blue**

KILLA KOUNTY 1-5
TENDER
By **Khufu**

MOBBED UP 1-4
THE BRICK MAN 1-5
THE COCAINE PRINCESS 1-10
STEPPERS 1-3
SUPER GREMLIN 1-4
A GANGSTA'S SON
By **King Rio**

MONEY GAME 1&2
By **Smoove Dolla**

THE DIRTY SIDE OF MONEY | PRINCE

A GANGSTA'S KARMA 1-5
By **FLAME**

KING OF THE TRENCHES 1-3
By **GHOST & TRANAY ADAMS**

BAD BITCHES WIT GUNZ 1&2
PROBLEM SOLVED
By "Christopher Diesel" Hornezes

QUEEN OF THE ZOO 1&2
By **Black Migo**

GRIMEY WAYS 1-3
BETRAYAL OF A G
By **Ray Vinci**

XMAS WITH AN ATL SHOOTER
By **Ca$h & Destiny Skai**

KING KILLA 1&2
By **Vincent "Vitto" Holloway**

BETRAYAL OF A THUG 1&2
By **Fre$h**

COUNTDOWN OF A KILLA 1&2
SEX, MURDER AND GOD 1&2
GUNS DOWN, BOTTOMS UP 1&2
By Lo-Life

THE MURDER QUEENS 1-7
By **Michael Gallon**

FOR THE LOVE OF BLOOD 1-4
By **Jamel Mitchell**

THE DIRTY SIDE OF MONEY | PRINCE

HOOD CONSIGLIERE 1&2
NO TIME FOR ERROR
By **Keese**

PROTÉGÉ OF A LEGEND 1,2&3
LOVE IN THE TRENCHES 1&2
By **Corey Robinson**

THE PLUG'S RUTHLESS DAUGHTER 1&2
By **Tony Daniels**

BORN IN THE GRAVE 1-3
CRIME PAYS
By **Self Made Tay**

MOAN IN MY MOUTH
By **XTASY**

TORN BETWEEN A GANGSTER AND A GENTLEMAN
By **J-BLUNT & Miss Kim**

LOYALTY IS EVERYTHING 1-3
CITY OF SMOKE 1-3
By **Molotti**

HERE TODAY GONE TOMORROW 1&2
By **Fly Rock**

WOMEN LIE MEN LIE 1-4
FIFTY SHADES OF SNOW 1-3
STACK BEFORE YOU SPLURGE
GIRLS FALL LIKE DOMINOES
NAÏVE TO THE STREETS
By **ROY MILLIGAN**

PILLOW PRINCESS
By **S. Hawkins**

THE DIRTY SIDE OF MONEY | PRINCE

THE BUTTERFLY MAFIA 1-3
SALUTE MY SAVAGERY 1&2
By **Fumiya Payne**

THE LANE 1&2
By Ken-Ken Spence

THE PUSSY TRAP 1-5
By **Nene Capri**

DIRTY DNA
By **Blaque**

SANCTIFIED AND HORNY
by **XTASY**

BOOKS BY LDP'S CEO, CA$H

TRUST IN NO MAN
TRUST IN NO MAN 2
TRUST IN NO MAN 3
BONDED BY BLOOD
SHORTY GOT A THUG
THUGS CRY
THUGS CRY 2
THUGS CRY 3
TRUST NO BITCH
TRUST NO BITCH 2
TRUST NO BITCH 3
TIL MY CASKET DROPS
RESTRAINING ORDER
RESTRAINING ORDER 2
IN LOVE WITH A CONVICT
LIFE OF A HOOD STAR
XMAS WITH AN ATL SHOOTER